Some Side Effe
A Feminizi
Blue Label Version

CW01501808

Part One

by Ann Michelle

ISBN: 9798386020910

Please visit my website:
www.annemichellesworld.blogspot.com

Ann Michelle

Introduction by Ann 3

Prologue..4

Chapter One: "A Tiny Prick" 5

Chapter Two: "That's Strange" 10

Chapter Three: "Being Frank At Work".........15

Chapter Four: "Am I Seeing Things?" 27

Chapter Five: *"You Did What?!"* 32

Chapter Six: "Don't Come" 40

Chapter Seven: "We're Not Hiding Away".......47

Chapter Eight: "Try This On" 57

Chapter Nine: "Unexpectedly Erotic" 67

Chapter Ten: "A Hard Day"...........................73

Chapter Eleven: "Poker Night" 84

Chapter Twelve: "Hiding It" 101

Chapter Thirteen: "More Problems" 107

Chapter Fourteen: "Martha Struggles".........112

Chapter Fifteen: "A Gift" 121

Introduction by Ann
— o —

Dear Readers,

Frank is an impulsive guy. One day, he learns about a new shot that is supposed to give him an extra inch down in the, uh, manhood department. Frank's wife Martha is a doctor who knows that anything making that kind of promise is probably not going to be safe. She absolutely forbids him to do it. But Frank, well, Frank does it anyways. Soon the changes start... but they aren't the changes Frank expected.

This is how Frank gets his manhood to grow an extra inch, but turns himself into a woman in the process as his wife gently reminds him, "I told you so." This is part one of the Blue Label version of this story, so expect Frank to get a little closer to some of the men in his life as well.

I hope you enjoy Frank's story! Let me know what you think!

With love,
Ann :)

Prologue
—o—

Her husband glanced at her nervously. Then he slowly lowered himself to the floor before the other man, which was anything but easy in the tight pencil dress and the sky-high heels. The other man stared down at him; there was an uneasy smile upon his face. The man reached down and raised his own dress, exposing a pair of silky white panties tented out by his own erection. The woman's husband took another deep breath. Then he cautiously pulled away the other man's panties, dropping them below the man's balls, and freeing his erection to the open air. He stared at the man's impressive erection pointing right at his lips. He swallowed hard... and hesitated. How had things gotten to this, he wondered?

"Go on," said his wife.

Chapter One: "A Tiny Prick"

—o—

Frank found his wife Martha pulling weeds from their raised flowerbed in the garden. She wore a yellow summer dress and white wedges. Martha was a doctor, a few months out of med school, who rarely dressed down, even for yard work. She said it gave her a sense of pride to always look nice and feminine.

"Did you see this?" asked Frank.

Martha looked up and wiped some soil from her cheek. She squinted in the bright morning sun.

"No, what is it?" she asked.

Frank held out a men's magazine. It was dog-eared to a page discussing a new drug. The drug had been developed by drug maker BioPharmaCon for the purpose of enlarging the male member. The drug was in the FDA approval process and certain doctors had just been cleared to prescribe it on a limited basis to aid in the study of the drug's effects.

"They have a shot now which is supposed to increase the size of a guy's dick by 15% in just a month," said Frank.

Martha stared blankly at her husband. "So?"

"So 15% would mean almost another inch. That would be amazing."

"*Frank*," said Martha in a tone of extreme disapproval.

"No, no, hear me out, Martha. Think of how much better our love life would be if I was an inch bigger! It's supposed to add girth too. Think about that. It could be thicker and longer."

"I'm not unhappy now, Frank."

"But it could be *bigger*, baby!"

Martha pursed her lips. "You men and your obsession with size! And what are the side effects?"

"There aren't any. That's what they said."

"That they know of *yet*."

"Maybe, but so far there's nothing, and it could add another inch!" said Frank excitedly.

"Or it might make your dick fall off. Or it might kill you. Frank, new drugs are dangerous. Until they've been used by thousands of people for years, there's just no way of knowing—"

"*But it's an inch!*"

"You don't need another inch," said Martha, and she held up her pinky finger to demonstrate how minor an inch was.

"Every man needs another inch."

Martha glared even more harshly at her husband. She loved her husband, but he had such a penchant for jumping at the too-good-to-be-true deal, and he never thought of the risks. This sounded dangerous to her. And truth be told, she didn't need him adding an inch to his manhood. She was satisfied. She didn't need more. And Frank? He didn't need more either.

"What if it makes you sterile? You know I want a baby," said Martha.

"Why would it?"

"Because you can't just make a dick grow an inch without making some serious changes to someone's hormones or DNA or who-knows-what? I don't think it's even possible."

"Martha."

"No, Frank."

"But honey—"

"*No*, Frank."

Frank sighed. His wife had spoken. He shouldn't have asked her; he should have just done it, he told himself. Now that she knew though, there would be hell to pay if he did it.

"I should have just done it," he grumbled to himself.

—o—

"Why did you even tell her?" asked Carl.

Carl was Frank's friend. They were at Carl's house watching the match and drinking beer along with Frank's other friend Ted. Frank had told them about the penis-growth drug and about his discussion with his wife. Carl and Ted had both moaned when they heard of Martha's disapproval.

"Because you don't just make decisions like surgery—"

"It's not surgery. It's just a shot," interrupted Ted.

"Same difference in this case," replied Frank as the good husband. "You don't just make decisions like this without consulting your wife. What happens if something did go wrong and you ended up in the hospital?"

"Or your dick falls off," laughed Carl, repeating Martha's comment.

Frank rolled his eyes. "Yes, or your dick falls off," said Frank sourly. "Either way, you can't do something like this without telling your spouse about it. And the fact you two cretins don't understand that tells me exactly what's wrong with your marriages." Frank put his beer to his lips and chugged.

"My marriage is fine. Ted's the one whose wife is 'Shtupping' the mailman," said Carl with a laugh.

"The 'mailman' is a lady," countered Ted.

"That makes it even worse."

"And who says 'Shtupping'?" asked Frank doubtfully.

"I saw it in a movie," replied Carl.

"Either way," said Frank again, "asking my wife was the right thing to do, so I did it."

There was a moment of silence as all three friends waited to see who would be the first to ask the question they all knew was coming next.

It was Carl. "So are you gonna do it anyways?"

Frank smirked. "Of course."

— o —

Frank knew there would be trouble if he went against his wife's wishes on this, so he did hesitate. He even told himself he would listen to his wife. After all, she was a doctor... a new doctor, but still a doctor. She should know about the dangers of drugs, right? But the idea of that extra inch gnawed at him day after day, hour after hour over the course of the next two weeks: an inch was huge in the world of penises and adding that inch would be... well, monumental. The idea dominated his brain. He thought about it at work. He thought about it at home. He thought about it while driving. It therefore came as little surprise to him when he found himself at the doctor's office staring at the consent form for the shot. He just couldn't resist.

Twenty minutes later, Frank was on his way home after a tiny prick in his arm.

His life would never be the same.

Chapter Two: "That's Strange"

—o—

Based on the article he'd read, Frank almost expected his penis to grow by the time he reached his car, but it hadn't. It hadn't grown by the time he got home either, or by the time he woke up the following morning. In fact, for the first four or five days, Frank noticed nothing at all. He didn't feel different and he didn't look different. As far as he knew, the shot had been a dud.

That was disappointing.

Then something strange happened, though Frank didn't connect it to the shot at first. He weighed himself, as he did every week, and he found he'd lost five pounds since the prior week. This was quite the surprise... quite the pleasant surprise! Not only had he never lost that much weight in a week before, but he wasn't even trying to lose weight, though he certainly could have stood to lose it. So losing five pounds was fantastic.

What caused it?

Well, Frank didn't really question it. He assumed it was all the "exercise" he was getting making love to his wife. She seemed particularly amorous recently, though Frank didn't know why, and they were making love almost every night. Whatever the reason, Frank was thrilled about the "exercise" and happy that he lost the weight. It seemed things were going well.

—o—

Wednesday's were poker night for the boys. Carl, Ted and Frank were at Ted's house drinking beer and playing cards. Meanwhile, their wives were at Frank's house doing whatever women do whenever they get together. Frank had the beginnings of a straight.

"So, did you get it?" asked Carl.

"Get what?" asked Frank as he rearranged the cards in his hand.

"The dick shot."

Frank chuckled. "So, so crude! Anyways, a gentleman never tells. Give me two." He tossed two cards at Carl, who dealt two back to him. Frank now held a pair of kings.

"Did it work?" asked Ted.

Frank shrugged his shoulders. "We'll see."

"That's a no," said Carl. "I'll take three." He dealt himself three cards.

"Give it time," said Frank.

"Yeah, a lifetime."

"Ye of little faith," replied Frank. At this, he laid his two kings on the table. Ted winced and tossed in his pair of tens. Carl, however, slapped down three queens; the winning hand.

"Queens over kings," said Carl.

Ted laughed and shook his head. "I thought he was bluffing. He had that look about him." He swallowed the rest of his beer. "Have you measured?"

"Measured what?" asked Frank.

"Measured *it*."

"It? Measured?"

"Yeah," said Carl. "Measured. Like gotten a ruler and measured." Carl collected the cards and started to shuffle the deck. "How do you know if the shot worked if you don't measure it? You can't just eyeball something like that to decide if it got bigger or not."

"I'm not measuring my dick, weirdo," laughed Frank.

"Then how do you know?"

"That's a good point," said Ted. "I doubt I'd even be able to spot an inch, much less something smaller when it just got started."

"Oh you'd spot an inch," said Carl as he handed Ted the deck to cut it.

"You think so?"

"Sure. In your case, an inch would double its size."

"Ha ha," said Ted sarcastically.

"What I want to know," interjected Frank, "is how he knows how big your doodad is?"

"You know, this conversation has really gone off the rails. Let's talk about women instead of measuring each other's dicks," said Carl. He started dealing.

The conversation moved on after that. But what his friends had said made sense to Frank. He realized he would never know if the shot had worked if he didn't measure his member. So when he got home, with the girls still in the kitchen giggling about something or other, Frank snuck off to the bathroom, surreptitiously grabbing a wooden ruler from the living room on the way through, and he measured himself. To do it, he stroked himself until he got as hard as he could get it and then he slid the wooden ruler along the top of his erection to the base. He placed his finger on the tip and looked at the number.

"That's my starting point," he decided.

— o —

Later that night, as Frank helped his wife clean up after the girls left, he got his second warning that something was not entirely right. He was putting away the dishes as his wife poured a pot of soup into a different container. He'd done this a thousand times without the slightest difficulty. When he reached up to put the plates in the cabinet this time, however, he was overcome with the strangest sense. It was like a cross between *deja vu* and that feeling when you know someone's been in an empty room. It was ephemeral and unreal, yet disorienting, and it made him swoon.

"Are you all right?" asked Martha, who saw him start to sway left to right.

"I— I'm ok," he said, recovering fast.

"What happened?"

Frank shrugged his shoulders. "Just turned my head too fast, got dizzy. Nothing to worry about." Frank wasn't telling the truth, however. The truth would have sounded too ridiculous. The truth was that when Frank reached up to set the plates into the cabinet his whole perspective seemed wrong to him, which triggered a sort of mini-vertigo. What was wrong with his perspective? Oddly, he'd felt smaller somehow, like everything was farther away and larger than it should have been.

"It was like I was seeing the world from a different angle... like I had shrunk just a bit," he would later explain. For now though, he shook it off and assumed it had been some trick of his mind or some such thing.

As much as Frank told himself this had all been a trick of the mind, however, he began to feel a little funny after this incident. Indeed, as he went about his day the next day, everything seemed "off" somehow: his clothes fit just a little poorly, as if they were a hint too loose. When he got in the car, the pedals seemed just a smidge further away than normal. And when he sat down, the table seemed oddly uncomfortable, like it had been raised just a hair. Everything was just a little... off. It was hard to put his finger on it precisely, but everything seemed out of proportion.

Chapter Three: "Being Frank At Work"

—o—

"Come on, Frank. I don't have all day," said Jade coldly. She was a waitress at *Empirey*, where Frank worked as a bartender and as the assistant manager. Frank hadn't started out to be a bartender; he initially went to school to learn marketing. But as he started college, he simultaneously got a job bartending to pay the bills. He was shocked to discover that he could make a lot more money doing that than working for a marketing firm. So while Martha continued on to medical school, he dropped out to become a bartender. Martha had always looked down on that decision, but he made more money than she did as a starting doctor, especially as a general practitioner. So in Frank's mind, he won.

"I can only pour so fast," replied Frank. Jade annoyed him.

"Well, pour faster."

"If you think you can do better —"

"You know I can."

"And yet, I have the job," said Frank in a tone sarcastically suggesting this was some mystery for them to contemplate.

"That's because William's sexist," said Jade contemptuously. The restaurant/bar manager, William, definitely had some "old school" views, as William described it. Frank didn't see a problem with it though as it didn't affect him.

"Some of us just have the skills," countered Frank.

That he did.

Frank grabbed the gin and the ginger. He knew this drink like the back of his hand. In fact, he knew most drinks, and what he didn't know, he had a real knack for creating. That's what got him the job at *Empirey. Empirey* was the swankiest bar in town. It was the kind of place that was stylized 1930's-hip done modern. The walls were rich woods, the chairs leather, and the booths secluded. The menu was high end and so was the alcohol. The waitresses wore real cocktail dresses and genuine high heels. The dresses had to be black, emerald, silver or gold to match the bar's theme colors. The waiters wore jacket-less tuxedos with white aprons, silver or gray vests and black bowties. They were required to wear cufflinks. As a bartender, Frank needed to wear a tailored gray or silver vest with a pocket watch chain, cufflinks on his starched white dress shirt, and black dress pants. He wore a narrow black tie tucked inside his vest. Tonight was another packed house, filled with young professionals demanding all sorts of special dinners and exotic drinks. The fact Frank knew how to make them all made him a real asset.

Frank finished three of the four drinks Jade ordered. She pulled them closer. Then she looked him up and down, with a confused expression on her face. "Have you lost weight?" she asked.

Frank ignored her and finished the final drink. He slid it to her. "Here."

"'bout time," said Jade, who was not one of Frank's fans either. She thought he was arrogant and sexist, like William their boss, whom she resented for making the waitresses wear heels. She'd tried to get William to change that, but when she asked Frank for his support, Frank merely laughed and said, "That's part of being a girl." When she stormed off, he condescendingly added, "look at that ass shake" as she walked away. She'd never forgiven him that, or forgotten.

Jade picked up the drinks and tottered off.

William appeared.

"How are things going?" asked William, who came around the bar to get himself a soda. He wore a black suit and a gangster-style tie. His gray hair was combed back in a wave.

"We're packed tonight," replied Frank. "Good crowd too."

William sipped his drink and watched Jade's rear as she worked her way toward a table. "That is one gorgeous woman. Crazy pain in my ass, but gorgeous. You could learn a lot about yourself from a woman like that."

"Just don't cross her," said Frank.

Like William, Frank watched Jade's rear shake as she disappeared around the corner. It was perfect. Not that Martha's rear was anything less than amazing, but Jade's rear was inspired. His penis started to grow watching her wiggle. Then something interesting happened. Frank suddenly had the uncanny feeling that his penis was growing bigger than it normally grew. In fact, it seemed larger than it ever had! His eyebrow shot up in surprise. Could the shot finally be working? Could this be it? Curiosity filled him. He wanted to know! No: he *needed* to know! But he knew he couldn't very well whip it out behind the bar and measure it. He would need to wait until he got home. He was suddenly very excited.

"Did you know she wants to be a bartender?" asked William.

Frank snapped back to reality. He shrugged his shoulders; he knew... *everyone* knew... she told everyone. "So make her a bartender."

"I'm not making a woman a bartender."

"Why not?"

"Old time superstition," said William dismissively. "Women don't belong behind bar."

"That's 'on ships', boss."

"And bars."

Frank shrugged his shoulders indifferently and reached for a twenty-year-old whisky. This wasn't his problem either way, he'd decided. "William and Jade can work it out," he'd long ago told himself.

"Besides," added William, "whose shifts am I going to take away to make that happen? Do you want to give up yours?"

"I hear she's an excellent *waitress*," laughed Frank by way of an answer.

— o —

When his shift ended around midnight, Frank raced home. He was excited! When he got there, he snatched the ruler from the living room cabinet and hurried to the bedroom; his wife was already asleep, so he slipped into the bathroom, where he stripped off his vest and dropped his pants and underwear. He needed to be hard for this, so he closed his eyes, thought about Jade's rear, and started stroking himself. His penis was rock hard within seconds, though oddly it almost seemed to Frank that it took more work to make it hard this time. Either way, it was now fully hard and he slapped the ruler down along the top of his erection.

"It's bigger!" he gasped. "It is!"

And so it was. It was a quarter inch longer than the last time! That was probably within the margin of measuring error, truth be told, but Frank didn't care. To him, the proof was undeniable. It had grown! The shot was working! Frank was elated. Not only would his manhood soon be a full inch longer, but once again, he had been proven right.

"We'll see if Martha objects now," he chuckled.

Frank tossed the ruler aside and stripped off the rest of his clothes. He decided to take a shower before bed. A good shower would hit the spot, he thought.

A few minutes later, Frank stepped under the stream of hot water. It washed over him, rinsing away the day, and relaxing him. When he was deeply relaxed, Frank put shampoo in his hair and then conditioner. Then he grabbed the soap and lathered it up in his hands before rubbing it over his chest. He'd done this a million times and knew what to expect. Only, when he did it this time, his nipples popped up; first his right nipple and then his left. They actually popped up! That had never happened before. And it felt strange. Normally, his nipples felt no different when he touched them than when he touched any other part of his chest. They were skin, that was all. But this time, he felt a very faint tingle when he pressed his nipples. What's more, his nipples felt oddly uncomfortable poking out, much in the same way that wearing jeans without underwear felt uncomfortable when his penis touched the denim material. Indeed, as the air and water passed over his nipples, they felt almost prickly... kind of like he imagined women felt when their nipples got hard.

Suddenly embarrassed by associating this feeling with women, Frank put his fingers on his nipples and pressed them back down. When he let go, however, they popped right back up. He tried again to push them down. This time, he grabbed the flesh around his right nipple and puffed it up before pushing the nipple back down into the flesh. As he did, he realized there seemed to be more flesh here than there had been before. Strange. It was like his chest had gotten puffy or flabby, but only behind the nipple. What's more, when he let go again, the flab didn't simply fade away, it seemed to stay on his chest, like a tiny mound just beneath the nipple. The other nipple looked the same as well. In fact, if he didn't know better, he would have said these mounds looked like the beginnings of breasts!

Breasts?! The thought burned Frank with embarrassment. Men did not have breasts and so he did not have breasts. This must all be some kind of mistake. It couldn't be real.

"This has to be my imagination," he told himself.

But was it? And why would he imagine having tiny breasts in any case? Frank didn't know for sure. It was all very strange and troublesome. He decided to double check; no doubt there had been a mistake. But when he moved his shoulders before he could check, everything redistributed a bit and the puffiness seemed to recede. Maybe it was just flab after all? Perhaps it had gathered together when he squeezed it? Maybe. Maybe the salt on the peanuts he ate or something made him retain water? Maybe. Maybe the hot water in the shower caused his skin to swell? Maybe. He wasn't sure. One thing he did know: he wasn't going to tell anyone about this. Fortunately, it had gone away again and he could pretend it never happened.

—o—

Two days later, Frank had an even greater shock. Frank and his wife were in their bedroom. Frank had stripped himself naked except for his socks, which he was working on pulling off. Martha lay on the bed in a silky black negligee. It was open, revealing her gorgeous breasts and toned stomach. She wore lacy black thong panties as well. He and Martha had gotten into the habit of making love almost every night of late. Frank didn't know what had turned Martha on so much, but he wasn't complaining. This night was no exception.

"Those socks are taking a long time," complained Martha playfully.

"They're resisting," replied Frank as he tugged on one.

"Is that the problem? I was starting to think you didn't want to play." As she said this, she ran her hand over her right breast and gently rubbed her nipple with two fingers, circling it in a figure eight.

Frank shuddered in anticipatory pleasure and gave the sock a great yank, making it fly off and land across the room. "*Wallah!*" He then slid onto the foot of the bed and crawled up between his wife's legs until his body rested on top of hers. She felt his erection press against her thong, tickling her lips beneath. He was hard as a rock. In fact, he was sure his penis was bigger yet, though he wasn't sure if it was enough for Martha to notice. Part of him hoped she noticed, part hoped she did not.

"Well hello," said Martha.

"Long time no see," replied Frank. He kissed her lips.

Martha kissed him back. She then wrapped her legs around Frank's hips. She felt Frank adjust himself so that his erection pressed right against her. His left hand went down and moved her thong aside.

"I love your panties," he said.

"I know," she purred back.

Frank used his hand to guide his stiff manhood inside her. *Would she notice,* he wondered? If so, she didn't say. "Give it time," he thought. He pressed it a little deeper and then brought his hand up to her chest and massaged her right breast, playing with her nipple as he slowly started moving in and out of her.

Martha shuddered at the dual feeling of having her breast played with and her husband's manhood inside her. It was exquisite! All her nerves were afire. Then Frank lowered his head and gave her nipple a quick lick with his tongue. She felt herself flush when he did this. Next, he gave it a gentle pinch. For as small of a pinch as it was, it stung and made Martha wince in a good way.

"Ouch!" she exclaimed as a wave of pleasure wash over her.

"You like that, don't you?" asked Frank.

Martha coyly shook her head.

"Yes, you do," he said confidently.

She shook her head again and giggled like a

school girl. Then an evil glint appeared in her eye. Without warning, Martha gave her husband one great shove and unexpectedly flipped him over onto his back on the mattress as she simultaneously rolled on top of him, pinning his arms to the bed. She now sat above him with her legs on either side of him, her arms pinning his, his erection inside her and her hair falling down into his face."

"Let's see how *you* like it, Mister!" she laughed.

Frank opened his mouth to issue a faux protest but Martha thrust her mouth at her husband's chest, landing her lips around his nipple, before he could speak. She snapped her teeth shut, biting his nipple – gently, but still with pressure – and pulling it away from his chest.

It shouldn't have hurt. It had never hurt before.

Yet, the effect was stunning!

Frank had never felt so much... shock... pain... thrill? He had no words to describe it. It didn't quite hurt, though there was certainly pain mixed in, but what he felt was intense and impossible to bear. It was like an overload feeling, like the time Martha had tried to tickle the head of his penis with her nails and nearly sent him clinging to the ceiling. It hadn't really hurt so much, but the thought of it hurt; it was like being hit with an electric jolt!

All of Frank's muscles instantly tensed. He instinctively tried to jump back, but with his wife on top of him and his back against the mattress, there was nowhere to go. Instead, he grasped the sheets and gritted his teeth as he struggled to bear this unbearable shock. He thought he might scream, but instead, he winced and writhed beneath his wife, clawing the sheets as she giggled at her naughty attack.

She pulled a little harder.

Frank gasped for air and arched his back. Anything more and he would lose control. He would throw her off and curl up into a ball. But then, just as suddenly as the "attack" began, it ended. His wife giggled, let go of his nipple with her teeth, and gave it a strong lick which made him come and collapse.

She had bitten him only for a few seconds in total, but it felt like hours to Frank. And the pressure she used would barely have been enough to register on his arm or leg or belly, but it felt like a thousand needles.

He was shocked!

"What was that?!" gasped Frank to himself.

Martha giggled once more and sat up, unaware of what had happened to her husband. She began moving her hips up and down, giving Frank a comparative break. She rode him for only a few seconds more before she finished. She then leaned forward, kissed her husband on the lips and went to the bathroom to shower for bed, leaving Frank lying there spent and stunned.

"I— what—?" That was all he could manage.

—o—

As Frank lay in bed that night, he tried telling himself that what he thought had happened hadn't really happened. It had all been a misunderstanding. He had been lying funny on his back when his wife touched him. That was all. It had been a mistake in perception. At most, he had somehow pinched a nerve or something, nothing more. But deep down, he worried that it had been something more. He worried about the flab. He worried the "flab" didn't look like normal flab; it looked more like solid tissue. It looked like little mounds under his nipples, not just a layer of fat spread across his chest. It wasn't swelling. And he hadn't done anything to get flabby either. To the contrary, he'd lost five pounds, hadn't he?

"Could it be five pounds of muscle?" he wondered.

How could he lose muscle?

That could be a problem, couldn't it?

He worried too that his nipples had become so sensitive. He'd never experienced that before. They stood up so strangely too. That only ever happened in the cold, not in a hot shower, and even then, they never felt annoyed when they stood up before. But most of all, he worried that he hadn't responded like someone shocked by a pinched nerve; he'd responded like a woman in heat. He'd pinched his wife's nipples before and he saw how she responded, the moaning and the breathless wincing and the writhing; he'd done the exact same thing. Something wasn't right. Men didn't respond that way.

But what was it? And what could be causing it? He hadn't done anything unusual lately. He hadn't eaten anything unusual. Nor had he been sick either. He hadn't gotten a massage or worked out that part of his body. Just about the only unusual thing he could think of was—

"*The shot.*"

Oh oh.

Frank bit his lip. Could that be behind this

somehow? Noooo. It couldn't be. The shot was doing the exact opposite, wasn't it? Hadn't it made his dick *bigger*? Why would a shot that made him more manly – made his dick grow – make his br— *chest* grow? That made no sense, right? It couldn't be that, could it?

What if it was?

Frank swallowed hard. It seemed he might have a problem.

Chapter Four: "Am I Seeing Things?"

—o—

Martha knew nothing of what Frank was experiencing and she had no idea what he was starting to suspect. To her, everything seemed normal. That was about to change, though.

It was Wednesday.

Martha pulled into the driveway. She was distracted. She'd been working at the new clinic now for several weeks and a problem had arisen. The problem was the doctor who ran the group: Dr. Martin. Despite Martha being married, and a woman, Dr. Martin kept hitting on her. *Hitting on her!* Dr. Martin. Dr. *Amber* Martin! A woman. Martha should have told her she wasn't interested in women and to never touch her again, yet, she hadn't. Why hadn't she? That was the question. She told herself she hadn't spoken up because she didn't want to lose her job, but that wasn't the real reason. The real reason, the one she didn't want to admit, was a bit more complex.

So rather than tell her off, every time Amber brushed up against her or put her hand on Martha's arm or shoulder, Martha found herself blushing like some silly school girl and tingling all over. Then she'd spend the rest of the day burning with arousal. Honestly, if she hadn't been able to relieve the tension this caused by making love to Frank, she might even have—well, who knows? Fortunately, having sex with Frank was keeping it in check.

Speaking of sex, she glanced at the clock. Frank would be going to work in two hours. That gave them just enough time for a quickie. Martha got out of her car and walked into the house. She set her purse on the table in the foyer and dropped her keys next to it. She kicked off her designer heels and pulled off her coat. She could hear the shower going.

"Frank must be showering," she said.

It stopped.

"And he's done. Perfect timing!"

Martha picked up her heels and started toward the bedroom. She thought about getting naked while Frank dried himself off and then surprising him in the bedroom; or she might put on some sexy lingerie. Either way, she knew what she wanted... what she needed. She was so incredibly horny right now. She could still feel Amber Martin's hand where it "accidentally" brushed against her breast while they were chatting in her office. That had made her wet.

Martha started toward the bedroom with her heels in her hand. In her stocking-covered feet, she made no sound as she approached the bedroom. As she reached the bedroom door, however, she saw the back of what appeared to be a naked woman walking away from the bathroom toward Frank's closet. The woman had wide hips, a narrow waist, and a jiggly rounded rear. Martha was stunned. Who was this woman?! *Why was she in Martha's house?!*

"Who are you?!" demanded Martha.

The "woman" turned around... it was Frank. Martha jolted. Then she stared at him in shock. How had she mistaken her husband for a woman? That seemed impossible, yet she had. How had she seen a feminine shape? Frank didn't look like a woman. How had she seen the hips, the rear, the hourglass shape? Could it be some sort of psychological thing because

Amber Martin was a woman and Martha apparently wanted her? "Latent Lesbian Desire" or some such thing? Martha bit her lip. Could this Amber situation be even more serious than she thought?

"Oh hi, honey," said Frank, apparently assuming her demand had been meant as a joke. "How was work?"

Martha forced a smile upon her lips and stepped into the bedroom. Once there, she did her best to examine his body without looking like she was looking. The feminine shape she had seen was gone. It was Frank. Just Frank. He looked a little "soft" perhaps, but there was really no reason to confuse him with a woman, especially with his penis swinging between his legs. Martha decided not to say anything lest Frank think she was going crazy or became insulted or that somehow led to the mention of Dr. Martin; Amber was the last thing Martha wanted Frank to know about.

"Nice shower, darling?" she asked absently.

"Very," said Frank and he kissed his wife on the lips.

As he did, a strange feeling came over Martha. It was as if something was off. Somehow, Frank seemed smaller... shorter... lesser? The feeling passed quickly though and she attributed it to her doubts regarding Amber Martin. In fact, it seemed crazy to her now to think her husband looked feminine or smaller or whatever. She returned his kiss. After that everything seemed normal again.

But this was only the beginning.

—o—

Later on, Frank was getting dressed for work. He'd put on his dress shirt and briefs and attached his cufflinks. He wore black socks and had just pulled his pants up to his waist. They were a little loose, so he tightened his belt a notch. Then he grabbed the suit-vest he wore and he slipped it over his arms into place. The vest normally fit his shape snuggly. Today, it really didn't.

It seemed oddly loose around his waist and shoulders.

Frank turned from side to side in the mirror. The vest looked wrong to him. It felt wrong too, too roomy. How could this be with his chest getting flabbier though? His pants felt loose as well, hadn't they? Maybe just a little. They lay funny over his shoes too. It almost looked like he hadn't pulled them up all the way and now they sat on the tops of his dress shoes.

"I must have lost more weight," he decided cautiously.

Then he wondered: could this all be related somehow?

He shook his head. It couldn't be. That made no sense. Besides, what happened the other night was just something strange. A one-off. It meant nothing. His clothes not fitting? It had to be the weight he lost, that was all.

"There's always a simple explanation," he said aloud as if trying to assure himself. "There's nothing more to it."

So why couldn't he get it out of his head that there was?

—o—

Over the next two weeks or so, both Frank and Martha noticed more changes. They were subtle changes though and each tried to ignore them or dismiss them. Frank dismissed these changes as just being the result of losing weight, though he wasn't even trying to lose weight, and he decided he was just feeling guilty and paranoid about taking the shot without Martha's approval. As for Martha, anything she noticed she attributed to mind games being played by her brain's inexplicable desire to go further with Amber – in fact, Amber seemed to sense the opportunity and had stepped up her touching and flirting. She had even brushed her hand against Martha's rear, supposedly by accident, as they left an elevator; each of these instances kept making Martha hornier and hornier, which made her feel guilty. Neither one wanted to believe what they saw. All that was about to change, however.

Chapter Five: *"You Did What?!"*

—o—

Frank leaned back as the waiter cleared his plate. He and Martha were at their favorite Italian restaurant, *Il Gorgio*. He wasn't as hungry as he normally was and left most of his food on his plate. That was probably why the wine seemed to affect him so much more than normal. All he'd had was one glass yet he definitely felt a little buzz! Strange.

"Are you ready?" he asked.

Martha nodded. She set her napkin down and rose to her feet. Frank did as well. He then took her hand and they walked out of the restaurant, with Frank holding the door open for her as they left.

"That was a lovely dinner," said Martha.

"I thought so too."

They moved together along the sidewalk, with each taking a different direction around a fireplug, still holding hands over it as they went. When they came back together, Frank glanced over at his wife and smiled. Martha turned her head to smile at him too. For an instant though, she felt oddly disoriented. She'd felt this before in recent days, but never so strongly. It was like her brain could not accept reality. But was it reality? Their proportions were off somehow. Different. In fact, it seemed that her husband was shorter. He couldn't really be shorter though, could he?!

Martha snuck a glance downward to assure herself that it was all an illusion; the sidewalk had to be lower on his side or something, or maybe she was wearing unusually tall heels and she had just forgotten.

But she hadn't... and it wasn't.

There was nothing unusual about her heels. She wore these rather often. They added perhaps four inches to her height and they did not make her taller than her husband. Tonight, though, they seemed to. He wasn't walking in a rut either; the sidewalk was level. There was no reason he should seem shorter, but he did. In fact, looking at him, he seemed somehow smaller all around too, though perhaps that was an illusion caused by his suit hanging loosely on him. Was this a new suit? Normally, his suits fit so well, but this one was way too large. It almost looked like he'd borrowed it from someone.

"Have you lost weight, darling?" asked Martha cautiously.

"Me? No, I don't think so," said Frank, forgetting the five pounds.

Martha furrowed her brow. Something wasn't making sense. How could he seem shorter and smaller? Why didn't his suit fit? He had barely touched his food too. Maybe he was dieting and didn't want her to know? Vanity?

They reached the car.

As Martha started around the car toward the passenger side, Frank grabbed his wife's arms and spun her around. He pressed her against the side of the vehicle. Then he pressed himself against his wife's body and dove in to kiss her neck. Martha's nipples popped up and she instantly became wet. Her chest started heaving. She leaned her head back to accept his kiss.

"Oh Frank," she purred.

Frank kissed her on the neck several times and

slid his hands down to her firm rear. He grabbed her butt through her silky black dress and squeezed. At the same time, Martha placed her hands on his ribs.

"What would people say?" giggled Martha.

"There are no people; I checked."

Frank pulled upward on her rear and kissed her lips deeply. Martha responded by sliding her hands up to his chest. She meant to press her hands against his chest to push him away in a sort of lover's tease, to add to the chase, as it were. Only, when her hands reached his chest, she felt something entirely unexpected. Rather than finding the flat, somewhat-toned chest she normally found, she seemed to encounter thick padding, as if her husband was wearing a padded bra. Even more incredibly, Frank jerked back harshly when she grabbed his chest and instinctively covered his chest with his arms as a woman might to protect her breasts. He was partially giggling and partially wincing as he seemed to cower before her. She'd never seen him act that way. In fact, it reminded her of a teenage girl's behavior more than anything!

"Are you all right?" she asked cautiously.

Frank clenched his teeth together and nodded. The shock of her nails catching his nipple had stung like fire and set off his nerves everywhere; he was hard as a rock and still tingling all over.

"I— I'm fine," he said.

"You don't look fine."

"It's nothing. It— it just tickled." The tingle ended.

Martha raised an eyebrow. Something was wrong and she knew it. Frank wasn't the ticklish type and he'd never responded like that when she'd touched him, not ever. She stepped closer. Frank imperceptibly stepped back. "Let me see it."

Frank shook his head. "It's nothing, really."

"*Let me see.*"

"There's nothing to see," he almost snapped.

It was too late for denials, however. Martha pushed him against the car as he had done to her. She reached for his chest, pushing aside his attempts to block her. She grabbed a handful of flesh on each side. There was no doubt it was flesh either; this was not some padded bra... it was him. It felt like two small breasts.

"*Frank!*" she gasped.

Frank's jaw dropped. His secret was out. "I— I can explain," he said with a weak smile.

"Get in the car."

— o —

"What is going on?" demanded Martha as they entered their home. They had driven in silence, both struggling with what was happening, each thinking about all the strange hints they had seen this week and questioning why their own guilt had kept them from seeing them.

"It's nothing," said Frank.

"Don't give me that, Frank," said Martha and she pitched her purse onto the table by their front door; something she did when she was deeply angry. She then ushered her husband toward the bedroom. Frank moved along helplessly.

"It's really nothing. Just flab," he said. Neither one believed that.

"That wasn't flab."

"I lost some weight," protested Frank.

"Losing weight doesn't cause *that*!"

Martha kept shooing her husband along with her hands and he kept retreating before her until they reached the bedroom. Martha moved her husband to the center of the room, where they both stopped and stared at each other, she in her little black dress and pumps, he in his oversized suit with the now-wrinkled shirt. She grabbed his jacket and started yanking it off. Frank tried to brush her hands away, but she was too determined.

"There's really nothing," he protested haplessly.

Martha didn't stop, however. She knew something was wrong. She knew what she'd felt. Not to mention, as crazy it might sound – as impossible as it seemed – she couldn't get it out of her head that he seemed... smaller. Even now, she was certain she was looking down into his eyes, something she had never done before. She pulled and twisted and yanked and Frank was spun and tugged in ways completely out of his control. A moment later, she had the jacket off and the shirt ripped open.

Martha gasped.

"You've got—!" Her eyes were transfixed on his chest where two small globes of flesh hung, globes that reminded her of herself as a teen. Suddenly, she recalled the day she came home from work and mistook him for a young woman: narrower waist, wider hips, fuller rear, curvy legs, reduced muscles; he'd looked like a girl going through puberty! "Have you been taking hormones?!" she demanded.

"Me? Wha— *no!*"

"Frank, be honest with me, are you taking hormones?"

Frank shook his head vigorously, which made his small breasts shake ever so slightly. "I swear, I'm not."

"How do you explain this then?" she asked sharply and she grabbed one of his breasts. He winced at the strength of her grasp and then writhed embarrassingly at the pleasure her touch sent racing throughout his body as she squeezed; his manhood instantly grew hard.

"It's just flab—"

"That's not flab, Frank!" She twisted his breast until he almost went down to his knees before letting go. She put her hands on her hips and glared at him. She wanted answers and those answers better be the ones she wanted to hear or she was not going to be happy. "What did you do?"

The question hung in the air for a moment. It seemed to echo throughout the room. Frank knew the tone meant she wouldn't give up. He had been caught and there was no escape.

"I mean it, Frank," demanded Martha once more. "No lies. You look smaller. Your shoulders, your waist. You look shorter, Frank. How is that possible? And now I grab your chest and find you're growing breasts? *Breasts?!*"

Frank cringed at the idea of growing breasts. It was humiliating. It was emasculating! He wanted to deny it. He opened his mouth to say whatever changes there were weren't that dramatic, that the flab could not really be called "breasts"... but as he did, he let go of his belt which was now looser than before as Martha had untucked his shirt. His pants took this very inopportune moment to crash to his ankles. Down they went, too fast for him to react. An instant later, he stood before his wife in baggy briefs, a wrinkled open dress shirt and little else.

His erection pointed right at her.

"Is this turning you on?" demanded Martha incredulously.

"No!"

It was too late to deny anything though; she had seen his erection. What's more, she was now staring at his shape in shock. There was the misplaced erection, yes, but other than that, it was all wrong. His hips looked larger than his waist and his thighs. That made them look more like women's hips than men's. His muscle definition was definitely reduced. His legs looked smaller and had a sort of curve to them which wasn't masculine either. And then there was his chest. *His breasts*.

"Frank!" she whispered in shock.

Frank cast his eyes to the ground. "I took that shot," he said in a defeated tone.

"Shot? What shot?"

"The one that's supposed to make your dick bigger."

Martha went silent. Her face turned bright red. She was angry. She was so very angry. She was so angry that Frank thought for a moment she might blow steam out her ears like in a cartoon. When she spoke, however, there was an ominous calm to her voice which made Frank cower in fear.

"The shot I warned you about? You took that one?" she asked.

Frank bit his lip and nodded.

"Even after I warned you that they hadn't done enough testing to know the side effects, you still took it?" Her tone remained steady... harsh, but calm.

Frank swallowed hard. "Yes."

"And that is what did this to you?"

Frank nodded his head.

"I see."

Frank opened his mouth to apologize, but he knew better. He said nothing.

Martha huffed out a deep breath. She glanced down at his crotch. "At least your dick didn't fall off," she said, her voice dripping in sarcasm.

Chapter Six: "Don't Come"
— o —

Frank stared at the tiled floor. He felt incredibly foolish. His wife's boss Amber, Dr. Amber Martin that is, had poked him, prodded him, examined his chest with his shirt off and felt him up. She'd squeezed his balls and pinched his mounds. By the time she finally told him to dress again, Frank felt like an object, not a person. When he was dressed, Dr. Amber, as Frank thought of her, drew his blood and asked them to wait as she tested the blood herself – it seemed better than letting some nosy lab technician conduct the tests.

"Are you sure she's good?" asked Frank as he buttoned his shirt. His chest felt heavy and created a slight bulge beneath his shirt.

Martha hesitated. Amber really was the last person she wanted to go to for help on this particular issue, or any issue really, because of what had gone on between them. But Amber was also one of the best hormone specialists in the country. If anyone could solve this, she could. And if it hadn't been for her "issue" with Amber, Martha would have recommended her wholeheartedly; in fact, she would have said there was no one better. So it made sense to bring Frank to her. She just hoped she didn't end up regretting this somehow.

"She's the best," said Martha truthfully.

"And she can keep a secret?"

She has so far, thought Martha. "Yes."

Frank nodded his head. After his wife discovered what he was hiding, she insisted on having him seen by an expert. She suspected it was a hormone imbalance caused by the shot which could be cured by hormone pills, but she wasn't sure which ones. That's where Amber came in. Frank hated the idea of telling anyone else what was happening to him, because it was embarrassing. But knew it was necessary. They had to stop this before it got worse! So he reluctantly agreed. And the fact his wife vouched for Dr. Amber, and assured him she could keep this a secret, helped immensely.

"I hope she knows what she's doing," said Frank nevertheless.

"Like you did when you took the shot?" sniped his wife. She was still upset Frank had gone behind her back and ignored her warning not to take the shot which had done this to him... *to them.* And she certainly didn't appreciate his questioning her medical judgment in picking Amber.

Amber soon returned with a long sheet of test results, which she slipped into Frank's file. She started writing notes about those results in the file as Frank and Martha sat side by side anxiously awaiting the verdict.

"It's really fascinating," said Amber finally.

Frank winced. That's a line he never wanted to hear from a doctor.

"Whatever that shot did to you, it's caused your body to produce a powerful and aggressive female hormone," she continued.

"How powerful?" asked Martha.

"Enough that it will slowly overwhelm Frank's male hormones and eventually remake him biologically as a woman."

Frank swallowed hard. He'd thought he was

maybe growing some fat on his chest... it was maybe a little breast-shaped, yes, but just misdirected flab. He had gotten fat. A simple diet, maybe some pills would remove it, right? And then he would be normal again. Maybe like his wife said, his hormones were a little out of balance. Nothing serious. Again some pills would that. That was not this. What did "remake him biologically as a woman" mean?

"I wouldn't call any of this 'slowly,'" replied Martha.

"No, definitely not," agreed Amber. "That's the strange thing. Biologically, this should be moving a lot slower and with much less effect. It should take months or even years to get this far. Something isn't normal." She paused. "I think I may know what's going on though."

"What's that?"

"You said your sex life is normal?" asked Amber. "How often would you say you've done it recently?"

Martha furrowed her brow, thinking this was perhaps an attempt by Amber to use this examination as some way to pry into her sex life with Frank; she felt oddly embarrassed at the idea of Amber knowing the details of her sex life. "What does that matter?" she asked defensively.

Amber held up her hand as if to say, "it does" and "stop being foolish." Martha realized she had overreacted and backed down.

"How recently do you mean?" asked Martha.

"Say the past week or two... since the shot," said Amber.

Martha blushed. Normal couples did it a couple

times a month, if that. Yet, she had been incredibly horny because of Amber lately so she and Frank had done it a lot more than that. She didn't want Amber knowing that, however, because Amber was smart enough to realize that their high rate of intercourse was the result of Amber's advances. That would be embarrassing if Amber found that out. She also worried that Amber might say something which would tell Frank that the reason they'd had all this sex was Martha's attraction to Amber. This would be bad too. But Martha also knew Amber needed to know the truth if she was going to solve this problem, and they needed to solve this before things got worse for Frank – they could get worse, right? That meant she needed to tell her.

"Probably every other night," admitted Martha softly.

"Or every night," corrected Frank.

Martha blushed.

"Interesting," said Amber. Her tone was clinical without a trace of suggestion, much to Martha's relief.

"So what is it?" asked Martha.

Amber held up her hand to hold off Martha's question for the moment still. She turned her gaze to Frank. "Have you noticed anything unusual after intercourse? Anything strange?"

"Like what?"

"Anything. A strange feeling. Emotional changes. Unusual soreness?"

Frank looked pensive. "I'm not sure, honestly."

Amber let out a frustrated breath; she'd clearly hoped for some concrete clue, but she didn't get it. She leaned back in her chair, folding her arms and crossing her legs. Like Martha, she wore short skirts, hose and high heels to the office. Like Martha, she was rather attractive too. She tapped her chin and appeared deep in thought.

"What is it?" asked Martha again.

"In their natural state inside Frank's body, the male hormones outnumber the female hormones by a good deal. That's what made him a man and keeps him a man," said Amber. "Flip that around and he would have become a woman."

She paused.

"Right now, in Frank's body, these new female hormones have a slight advantage—"

"Slight?"

Amber nodded her head. "Yes, slight. Just a tiny fraction of a percentage. It's enough that over a twenty or thirty year period, Frank would probably slowly develop the secondary characteristics of being a woman—"

"I'm turning into a woman?!" gasped Frank.

Amber shook her head. "Biologically – from a hormone perspective – yes, but not from the perspective you mean. You'll develop secondary characteristics only and they won't be truly feminine in form or function. Think gynecomastia. That's when males develop larger than normal breasts. They may be embarrassing to the young man, but they aren't especially feminine in shape or function. No one would mistake the young man for a woman, and he can't produce milk. If you flood a man with enough feminine hormones of the type you are getting from that shot, that is what you get: you get a male with secondary female characteristics, but not a female. In other words, it shouldn't actually turn you into a woman."

"What kinds of things are we talking about? What are secondary characteristics?"

"Breast tissue growth, reduced muscle mass, softer penis, loss of erections, less body hair but more lush hair. That sort of thing."

Frank twisted his lips nervously; that sounded pretty womanly to him. Not to mention, he was horrified at the idea of growing breasts of any sort. And the rest of it sounded terrible too. How soft? How much muscle? He wouldn't be able to get it up anymore?

"How— how long will that take?" asked Frank nervously.

"That's the thing. Given the levels of hormones, we're talking about decades, if at all." She paused before adding, "That's if these hormones continue to fight it out naturally."

"But something is helping them?" asked Martha.

Amber nodded her head. "Yes." She paused. "I think *you* are."

"*Me?!*"

"Both of you," said Amber.

"How?" demanded Martha.

"Every time you and Frank have intercourse, and Frank ejaculates, he essentially burns male hormones. If he hadn't ejaculated, those sperms would have melted back into his system and, to make this easy, added to his manhood levels. When he ejaculates them, that no longer happens. So each time he ejaculates, he loses male hormones which gives the female hormones a stronger advantage."

"So every time I come—" gasped Frank.

"You give the female hormones a day or two to run wild," replied Amber.

"So that means—"

"Have sex, become a girl." She'd said it straight up and clearly.

Frank's jaw dropped. He wanted to faint. They had been having sex every night! He'd come dozens of times since he took that shot. Had each one caused him to become more feminine?

"But how are female hormones making him shorter, smaller? That's not possible," protested Martha.

Amber shrugged her shoulders. "Not as far as we know. But apparently, it is. Or maybe it's just perception."

"But how?"

"This is an experimental procedure. It's full of proteins and reactants that aren't fully understood. Something within the formula itself is essentially re-writing his DNA on the fly to give him feminine characteristics, not masculine versions of secondary feminine characteristics, but actual feminine characteristics. That's the other interesting angle."

"You mean, he's really turning into a girl."

Amber nodded her head slowly.

"So what do we do?" asked Frank. His mouth was dry. He was sweating.

Amber shrugged her shoulders. "Don't come."

Chapter Seven: "We're Not Hiding Away"

—o—

"'Don't come.' What kind of advice is that?!" grumbled Frank. He turned the corner and accelerated the car toward their street. "'Don't come.' How is that the least bit helpful?" His tone was dismissive, angry, and yet, nervous.

"That's not all she said," said Martha, correcting him.

"That's all the advice she gave us *right now*."

"*Right now*, yes, because she doesn't have any answers yet. She needs to run more tests. Like she said, she thinks she can stop the process and maybe even reverse it with the right hormone cocktail, but she doesn't want to give you anything until she runs some tests and knows what to give."

"Can't we try *something* at least rather than wait and see what kind of damage this stuff does in the meantime?" said Frank sourly. The idea that he might grow breasts or might turn into a "biological woman" was alarming. He imagined himself with small breasts; it was humiliating.

"Would you rather she experimented and accidentally sped this up?"

Frank bit his tongue. "No."

"Or made it permanent?"

"Absolutely not!"

"Then trust her. She needs time."

"And what am I supposed to do in the meantime?"

"Don't come," said Martha drolly. To be fair,

Martha was worried about her husband for sure, but she couldn't help but feel a little *schadenfreud* about this too. She had warned Frank not to do this and he ignored her warning, as he always did. She was a doctor, and yet, he never took her advice seriously. This was all part of a pattern of disrespect she felt he showed her. It was therefore fitting, she thought, that he'd put himself in this position by ignoring her advice, and it was even more ironic that the danger he'd brought down upon himself was a threat to his masculinity, the same masculinity which made him think he knew more than her. "Maybe you should learn to listen to your wife," she thought.

"Ha ha," said Frank bitterly. "Don't come." He nearly spat the words.

"Don't blame me, Frank. You brought this on yourself. This is all on you. And until Amber finds a solution, you better do what she says and make sure you don't ejaculate."

"What if she's wrong?"

"What if she is?"

"Then I'm wasting my time trying to act like sex is going to kill me."

Martha stared at her husband in disbelief. "Are you serious? Is sex that important for you that you're willing to risk ending up a girl just so you can get off a little now and then?"

Frank blushed. He had embarrassed himself.

"Because that's what it sounds like, Frank," continued Martha.

"Fine," grumbled Frank. He could give up sex for the moment. Giving up sex was the least of his worries right now. Right now, turning into a woman was his biggest worry. He was also worried about how he was supposed to live his life with these budding traces of femininity! What if other people could spot them? How was he going to go to work looking like this? How could he see their friends knowing they might be staring at his chest or his hips or wondering if he didn't look a little... *soft*? The idea made him shudder, especially if it got worse as it sounded like it still might.

"I think I'm just going to hide at home until this all wears off... until she finds a way to reverse it," said Frank.

"Oh no you're not," said Martha.

"Why not?"

"For one thing, we need your income. My income is nice, but we based our lives on both of us working. That means you need to keep your job so we can pay our bills. To do that, you need to go to work. Also, I'm not having you turn into some crazy hermit who sneaks around the shadows of our house. Some jiggly Phantom of the Opera. You need to live your life normally. And I'm not giving up my life, our friends, and our time together just so you can hide your embarrassment at something that never should have happened."

"Now hold on —" said a nervous Frank.

"No Frank, that's how it's going to be," insisted his wife. Her tone struck Frank as surprisingly firm, almost commanding. It was clear he was not getting out of this, no matter how hard he tried.

"But people will see me."

"Yes, they will, and that's the price you need to pay for doing this. You got yourself into this, so I don't want to hear it. *We* are going to live normally. I'm not giving up my life because you're embarrassed. It's enough that I need to give up my sex life because of you."

"I'm not real thrilled about giving that up either," said Frank accusingly.

"Neither am I, Frank. I'm being punished for your mistake just like you are."

Frank groaned in response.

"I warned you, Frank. Didn't I say to avoid that shot? Didn't I tell you it had unproven side effects? Didn't I tell you it could make your dick fall off? But you couldn't listen to me, could you?"

"My dick didn't fall off," countered Frank snidely.

"Except it's unusable now unless I want to turn you into a woman, so it might as well have fallen off."

A chill raced down Frank's spine at his wife's quip, not only at the emasculating idea that his dick had become useless but he suddenly saw real danger. Indeed, he had a rather strange vision flash before his eyes in which his wife was deciding whether or not to turn him into a woman. She decided she would and she jerked him off until breasts sprouted on his chest. The vision made his stomach drop. She could do that to him at any time, making him as feminine as she wanted. This was an incredible power to hold over him. Did she realize she held this power? Would she use it if she did? He suddenly felt rather vulnerable.

"I still think— it just seems— it seems like it makes more sense to hide away," said Frank much more cautiously, suddenly a little afraid to anger his wife. "What if someone finds out?"

"Are you planning to tell people?" asked Martha incredulously.

"No! Of course, not."

"Then no one has any way to know, do they?"

"What if they do?" Frank turned into their driveway.

"Be reasonable, Frank," said Martha. She grabbed her purse. "Amber will solve it and no one will ever know. It will just take time. Now let's go inside and work on your wardrobe."

"My wardrobe? What about my wardrobe?" asked Frank.

"Nothing you have fits. Your pants fell when you let go of them. I watched you holding them up the whole time we met with Amber. Your shirt is so baggy it might as well be a tent."

"I need new clothes."

"You do," agreed Martha. "But new clothes are not in the budget."

"Then what are we going to do?"

"We're going to fix the ones you have. I'll take your clothes to Rosalie tomorrow. She can adjust them; she's the best seamstress I know. Apart from that... we'll make do."

— o —

A few minutes later, they were in the bedroom. Martha stood before her husband. She wore a dark skirt suit and heels and held a tape measure in her hand. Frank wore a white dress shirt and black slacks. He had his arms crossed over his chest self-consciously.

"Strip, Frank," said Martha.

Frank twisted his lips. "Do I need to?"

Martha shot her husband a disapproving glare. "Frank. I'm trying to help."

"Just measure me through the stuff I'm wearing."

"*Frank.*"

Frank pursed his lips. "Fine." He slowly unbuttoned his shirt and then pulled it off. As he did, his chest came into view, and with it, the two small mounds upon his chest. They looked like they belonged to a young woman just into the throws of puberty. They were small and shaped like amorphous mounds more than anything. That said, they did jiggle a bit as he bent over to pull off his pants. Martha was still shocked to see them, even though she'd seen these several times already. Her husband really truly was growing breasts!

The idea was shocking. It was actually kind of exciting too.

"I don't know what the big deal is," said Frank disingenuously, trying to rescue some masculine pride. He stepped out of his pants and underwear and bent over to pick them up. The mounds jiggled.

Martha watched them jiggle in utter fascination. As she did, she felt strongly compelled to touch them. Almost without realizing it, she cupped his right breast in one hand. Frank tensed up immediately before his muscles surrendered as a warm, pleasurable sensation radiated from her hand throughout his body. It made him weak and temporarily helpless.

"What are you doing?" asked Frank pensively, though he didn't push her hand away. It felt too good to do that.

Martha drew closer and squeezed her husband's breast around the nipple. It grew firmer and puffy in her hand like a balloon does as you squeeze it. This made his nipple shoot up too. His penis shot to attention as well. So did Martha's nipples, though Frank didn't know this.

"This is amazing," said Martha.

Frank closed his eyes. His breathing became harder.

Martha responded by kneading his breast like dough. She saw him writhe beneath her ministrations. His body trembled. Tiny gasps escaped his lips as they had hers the first time a man touched her breasts. His penis visibly throbbed. She had rarely seen it throb without being touched and it excited her to do that. It meant she had found something so exciting, so intense, so pleasurable that her husband was lost in her control. That turned her on in a strange new way.

She squeezed a little harder.

His penis stood even taller.

Martha became very wet. She wanted to push harder, to tug on his nipple, to run her tongue across his nipple, and to see him explode. She wanted to make him explode without even touching his penis. She could do it; she was sure of that.

But then, like a distant call, Martha heard Amber's words float through her brain. At first, they were a whisper but soon became a warning: *"Have sex, become a girl."* She needed to stop. She knew it. She didn't want to stop as this was intensely erotic, but she knew she needed to stop or something bad would happen. *"Have sex, become a girl."* It took considerable will, but she pulled her hand away.

"Don't stop," whispered Frank breathlessly.

"We have to... Amber.... the warning."

Frank snapped out of his erotic fantasy. He'd forgotten the danger. It seemed impossible, but he had forgotten. He took a deep breath and nodded his head. They needed to stop.

He sighed.

For the next several seconds, neither could look at the other. They were both shocked at what they had nearly done and at how excited each felt at what they were doing. Neither understood why this had been so exciting. Finally, Martha held up the measuring tape.

"Let's check your measurements," she said.

Frank nodded his head. Neither acknowledged what had just happened.

Martha ran the tape measure around her husband's chest. Her arms met behind his back much more easily than usual. He'd clearly lost size around his chest. She checked the tape measure.

"Your chest is 40 inches," she said.

"But my chest is —"

"I know." It was smaller; he'd lost muscle mass. She examined his chest with her hands, a little less sensually this time. She glanced at him from the side, wrapped her tape measure around the mounds, and then announced, "I'd say you're on your way to a B-cup too. Not yet, but starting."

"What does that mean?"

"B is more than A."

"But what does that mean?"

"It means you probably need to start wearing a bra," said Martha.

The shock of this statement stunned Frank. A

bra?! Had she said a **bra**?! The idea of wearing a bra was intensely emasculating, more so than anything that had happened to him so far. He was literally speechless for several seconds.

"Never," he said finally after gathering his composure.

Martha nodded her head in support, but did so doubtfully; he would need a bra, especially if there was any more growth. She let it go for now though and moved the tape measure down to his waist. "Your waist is forty-inches. No wonder your pants keep falling."

Frank blushed; he wore a 42. At least, he used to.

Martha slid the tape measure down to his hips. "Forty-one-inch hips. Average for a woman, above average for a man." This was an ominous statement to Frank as it meant it wasn't just his chest that was expanding. He really was slowly evolving into a genuinely feminine form. Martha then ran the tape measure around his neck. "And a fourteen-inch neck. Down an inch."

Frank swallowed hard. His neck was smaller?

"One more measurement," she said and she crouched down on one knee; her tight skirt barely let her do this. She jammed the tape measure into her husband's balls. Then she unrolled it down his thigh, down his calf, and to his ankle. She read the number to herself, but didn't tell Frank. He was dying to know, having worried that somehow he might actually be shrinking, but he felt too embarrassed to ask... *what if he really had shrunk*?

"I'll give these measurements to Rosalie in the

morning," said Martha.

Frank nodded his head. "What do we do in the meantime?"

Martha shrugged her shoulders. "We make dinner and go about our evenings. But first, why don't you gather the clothes you want me to take to Rosalie. Then we'll see if I can find something for you to wear in the meantime."

Chapter Eight: "Try This On"

— o —

Frank stared incredulously at his wife. She was holding up a pair of hot pink shorts. Women's shorts. *Hot pink.*

"You're joking!" he gasped.

"These will fit," she replied.

"I can't wear *those!*"

Martha glanced at the small shorts in her hand. "Why not?" she asked.

"They're *women's* shorts!" exclaimed Frank in a shocked tone as if the answer was so obvious he couldn't believe she didn't see it.

"So?"

"So, *I'm a man.*"

Martha didn't see the problem. Sure, they were pink and pink wasn't a manly color, but it wasn't like they were bootie shorts or a skirt. Besides, beggars can't be choosers and right now, this is all they had. "That may be, darling, but these are the only thing that fits you right now... unless you want to try on some of my dresses."

Frank's eyes bulged. *"Dresses?!"*

"Yes, darling, *dresses.* It's not a dirty word, and if your breasts—"

"*Chest!*" protested Frank.

Martha rolled her eyes. "All right. Chest. If your chest was any bigger, or your hips wider, that's what you would be wearing right now. You wouldn't have any choice in the matter because nothing else would fit."

"I will *never* wear a dress," declared Frank.

Martha glared at her husband. She was trying to remind herself that this must be difficult for him as indeed it was shocking even to her, but it was getting really annoying dealing with his insecurities. There was nothing they could do about this at the moment; his body no longer fit into his own clothes. She couldn't wave a magic wand and change that. Heck, they were lucky her shorts even fit him! Besides, shorts are shorts, what did it matter if these were labeled for women rather than men? It was time he got over this male pride thing!

She decided to explain it once more.

"These shorts are the only thing that might fit, so try them on," said Martha calmly. "Beggars can't be choosers."

Frank shook his head. "I'll find something of mine." He reached for the bag of clothes he had gathered for Martha to take to her seamstress friend in the morning.

"Stop, Frank."

"I can't wear women's shorts!" protested Frank.

"Frank, nothing you have fits. These will fit. Now put them on and stop being ridiculous. I'm getting sick of it," her calm was fading and her tone was becoming increasingly firm.

Frank gritted his teeth. Wasn't it bad enough he was growing breasts and whatever else had happened? Did his wife need to make this worse by suggesting he wear women's clothes too? He knew she was right – nothing else he owned fit him anymore – but *still*. The thought was humiliating. Women's clothes???

It took him a moment to calm himself and remind himself that it was only for one night. Rosalie would tailor his clothes tomorrow and then he could wear those again. But right now, his wife was right. His shirts hung on him like bags. His pants kept falling down even as they caught on his hips; not to mention, they caught under the heels of his shoes already if he wasn't careful. So it made sense. Still, the idea of wearing women's clothes, even something as minor as a pair of shorts was emasculating and he struggled badly with it.

"Put the shorts on, Frank," said Martha more firmly. She was tired of fighting against his ego for something this pointless. They were just shorts, they weren't the end of the world!

"I—"

"*Put them on*," she hissed.

Frank snatched the shorts. "If you ever tell anyone, I'll file for divorce," he grumbled hyperbolically.

"So be it," said Martha with some relief.

Frank unbuttoned them. He stared down into them like they were some sort of dangerous portal he was considering sliding into. Martha rolled her eyes at the drama he was making of this. They were just shorts after all. It wasn't like it was a ball gown and platform heels.

"Just slip them on?" he asked.

"Naturally. Just like your shorts. Although, you might want to put on underwear first."

"Why?"

"Do you normally wear pants without underwear?" asked Martha snidely.

Frank blushed. He realized he was making a fool of himself being so uptight. The reason he wore underwear was because having his penis rub against harsh materials, or Heaven forbid a zipper, was not a good idea; it wasn't some plot to emasculate him. So he went to his dresser drawer and he grabbed a pair of white briefs. He tossed the shorts onto the bed and stepped in the briefs, pulling them up his legs. They felt rather loose as he pulled them into place however, and the moment he let go of them, they slid right back down to the bottom of his cheeks and then fell down his legs all the way to his ankles.

He stared at them. "I guess those don't fit."

"I guess not," added Martha sarcastically.

"I guess I go without."

Martha shook her head. She marched over to her panty drawer and grabbed the first pair of panties on top. These were pink boy-cut panties with narrow lace trim. "Put these on."

"B— but those are p— panties," gasped Frank as a chill shivered down his spine. The idea of wearing women's shorts was hard to take, but the idea of wearing panties was somehow infinitely worse. Shorts were shorts, but panties... those were exclusively for women.

"*Frank*. You're already wearing women's shorts, what is the harm in wearing panties too? Stop being ridiculous."

"But they're for women—"

"Then it's good you're turning into one," said Martha irritably. "Stop fighting me on this and stop dragging your feet. Put on the panties and stop being such a little girl about it!" She shoved the panties into her husband's chest. He instinctively grabbed them.

Frank held the panties out before him and

slowly stepped into them. Then he pulled them up into place, feeling their silky smoothness slide along his legs. He prayed they wouldn't fit. Too small, too large, it didn't matter: just don't fit. But they fit perfectly. He felt sick.

"Now put on the shorts and let me see what else I can find that might fit you," said Martha.

As Frank helplessly slipped into the pink shorts, Martha scanned her closet for a top for her husband. As she did, she actually found herself skipping over the more gender neutral items in her wardrobe as a sort of punishment for Frank being so difficult about the panties and for causing all of this in the first place. She settled on a white top with spaghetti straps. It was very feminine.

"How are your shoes?" she asked.

"They're fine."

"Let me see you in them."

Martha turned to examine her husband's feet and got a shock. Her husband stood before her in the hot pink shorts, presumably with the panties underneath, shirtless and blushing. The shorts enhanced his feminine shape rather than hiding it, and made him look distinctly feminine. Indeed, they narrowed his waist, expanded his hips, and made his legs looks smaller. What's more, his breasts where starting to look like real breasts – had they been this big before? They weren't quite globes yet, but they looked like small pyramids of flesh that were rounded at the bottom by gravity. Interestingly, his areolas looked larger too and his nipples had grown from the size of the tip of a pencil to maybe double that size now. He looked like a teenage girl! This was the first time she noticed how feminine they looked. Strangely, this didn't upset her as she thought it would have. To the contrary, it kind of made her horny.

"I— uh," said Martha who had lost her train of thought from the unexpected horniness.

"They fit, trust me."

That brought Martha back on track. "Shoes. Yes, um, I want to see them. See you in them. I don't want you tripping." She realized she was becoming wet.

Frank scowled. This all seemed so needlessly embarrassing – in fact, he wondered if Martha might not be enjoying it all just a little bit too much at this point. Either way, Frank slipped his feet into his shoes to prove they fit. To his horror, he realized right away that they felt looser than they normally did. He wasn't going to admit that though as he knew where Martha was headed with this and the idea of wearing her shoes was simply unimaginable. Besides, they fit well enough.

"See, they fit," he said.

"Walk."

Frank rolled his eyes and started out across the room. The first step went well, as did the second. The third felt funny as the loose shoe seemed to shift on his foot. He spread his toes to hold it in place. As he did, his other foot left the ground for his fourth step, but the shoe did not. It stayed behind. Frank had literally walked right out of his shoe.

"They fit, do they?" said Martha sarcastically.

"They might be a little loose."

"Well, you can't go around in shoes that slide off your feet."

"They're fine," said Frank.

Martha ignored his protest. She turned back to the closet and grabbed a pair of dark red, almost-black loafers with an inch and a half chunky heel. These were women's shoes, but which she thought might not be noticed as such at a distance... *might*. "These are a little too big for me, but should fit you," she said. "Wear these."

Frank's jaw dropped. "Those are w— women's shoes!"

"I certainly hope so as I bought them for me. And now you can wear them."

"But—"

"I'm not having you fall and hurt yourself."

"Honey," protested Frank.

"Put on the loafers, Frank, or I'll find some heels. Then you'll really look like a girl."

Martha held out the shoes. Frank shrunk from them, but knew he had no choice. They had been over this already with the shorts and panties. He didn't like the idea of wearing anything feminine, least of all women's shoes, but he also realized his wife was right. Like his pants and shirts, his shoes just didn't fit. If he tried to wear those, he would spend the day struggling to keep them on his feet and would likely end up tripping from time to time. It was just smarter to wear the loafers. Besides, he assured himself, it was only for one day and they did kind of look like men's loafers.

"It could be worse," he told himself.

Frank snatched the loafers from his wife's hands. He tossed them to the floor before him and slid his feet inside them. Again, he hoped they wouldn't fit, but they did. Once more, he had no excuse to refuse.

"Perfect," said Martha.

"I'm only wearing these until we can get me smaller men's shoes," snapped Frank.

Martha rolled her eyes in response. "Put on the top." She held out the top she had grabbed from the closet.

"Shirt."

"Whatever, Frank."

Frank took the top and slipped it over his head. It fit. It was comfortable too. That said, the spaghetti straps made him shudder. Men didn't wear those. What really should have worried him though was his breasts. The top was made of a light and delicate material which became see-through in certain light, and his enlarged areolas were showing through rather clearly. Moreover, the top did nothing to hide his growing mounds. The only reason this didn't stop Frank dead in his tracks was that he couldn't see the top from Martha's angle. She saw it and she was struggling to suppress a giggle while simultaneously soaking her panties. She was highly, highly turned on by this, so much so she blushed and felt hot all over.

He moved to the mirror to examine himself. This angle didn't afford him the full view Martha had seen, but what he saw still felt wrong. He looked terribly non-masculine in this top.

"Don't you have a normal shirt?" he asked as he looked over his reflection.

Martha shook her head, still trying not to laugh or gasp. "Nothing that doesn't have ruffles or lace," she lied.

Frank pursed his lips. "Maybe I should just skip the shirt."

"*Frank.*"

"But it's so feminine."

"Just be glad I don't make you wear a bra. You probably need one actually," she said and she grabbed for his chest with her hand to make the point, though he ducked away. His chest jiggled embarrassingly as he did.

"I just don't like the idea of wearing women's clothes," he complained.

"Then you shouldn't have taken that shot," said Martha. She felt oddly dominant suddenly, like it was natural for her to take charge in this moment. Perhaps his feminized state was goading her into this. Perhaps, it was a little bit of payback for the way he'd acted in the past. Either way, she was in no mood to back down. "You were warned anything could happen, Frank. You brought this on yourself, and you're not going around half-naked just because my top embarrasses you. Besides, this is only until Rosalie takes in your clothes. I think you can manage wearing these things for a day or two until she's done, or aren't you man enough to handle that?"

Her taunt struck right at his insecurity. It also stripped him of any defense. He was beaten. So that was how things would be that day. Frank would walk around in the girly shorts, the very feminine top and the low-heeled loafers with his enlarged breasts showing through the top and jiggling ever so slightly. It would be a difficult emasculating day for him.

Martha, on the other hand, felt powerful. Frank never respected her or her opinions, but now he had no choice; she had the upper hand. That actually made her happy, in a way. It even made her a little wet. Not that she wanted any of this to happen to her husband – she did want him to be healthy and happy – but maybe, she thought, *maybe* a little bit of being emasculated like this would do him some good.

Chapter Nine: "Unexpectedly Erotic"
—o—

With his wife reading medical journals in the kitchen, Frank slipped away to the bedroom. His mind was spinning with much of what had happened. What exactly did it mean to become a biological woman? Was he really growing breasts? What would breasts look like on a man if they kept growing? What would happen to the rest of him? How bad could this all get?

Frank grabbed the laptop they both used for their online activities and sat down at his wife's vanity table. He opened an internet search page. He wanted to find out more about men growing breasts. The results returned, however, weren't quite what he'd expected. Rather than finding the results of clinical studies and articles by doctors, his first attempt returned a series of photos of men in women's clothes. Frank was just about to reset his search when one of them caught his eye.

Sunny.

"Sunny" looked to be a woman. A very attractive woman, in fact. But the header suggested otherwise.

"That can't be a man," said Frank dismissively.

Frank went to try a different search but stopped before he left the page. His curiosity had gotten the better of him. Could this "Sunny" really be a man? It didn't seem so. She was far too pretty, far too natural. There was no way *this* could be a man. So why had she come up on this search? Frank clicked on her page to find out. Her headshot came up.

"She's really pretty," said Frank to himself.

Ann Michelle

He was more certain than ever this was no man. There just weren't any traces of masculinity. He clicked on the link for a gallery page. The first photo that came up showed "Sunny" standing in her kitchen. She wore a black business suit with a knee-length skirt and simple pumps. She was holding an apparently heavy briefcase before her, as if she was struggling to keep it up. Her wavy blonde hair hung down over her shoulders and she was laughing. The front of her suit was open, as was the top of her blouse and considerable cleavage was showing. She had large, perfect breasts. She was very pretty.

"That is no woman. No way."

Frank clicked on the next image. This time "Sunny" wore a tight black dress that ran to the middle of her thighs. The dress had a heart-shaped collar which again showed considerable cleavage. Around her neck was a single strand of pearls in the form of a choker. Her legs were encased in tan stockings and on her feet were tall pumps with open toes. One hand pressed against her right breast and the other rubbed along her left thigh. It reminded him of a pose he'd seen in girly magazines when he was younger. He followed the curves of her breast and felt his penis start to stir.

"Definitely not a woman," said Frank with a laugh.

Obviously, the search result had misfired on this one.

Frank was just about to go back to his search when he saw the word "secret" written over one the pictures. The picture was blurred out. Frank's curiosity was piqued once more. He tapped the link.

Another picture of "Sunny" appeared. In this one, she'd unzipped the dress and let it fall down to her elbows, uncovering her breasts completely. They were held in a black lacy bra with little bows where the cups and straps met. Sunny had pulled her right breast from the bra's cup and it was hanging freely. It was large and round and firm and it had a swollen areola with a big pink nipple the size of a pencil's eraser. It was gorgeous. Her hand was teasing the erect nipple and she pressed against it with the tips of two painted nails. This was highly erotic.

But that wasn't the most interesting part of the photo.

As Frank continued to examine "Sunny," his eyes drifted further south. There, "Sunny" had hiked up her dress on one side exposing most of her panties at an angle. Incredibly, her thin panties seemed to be holding back something about the size of Frank's fist.

Frank froze. He was stunned.

"What is— no! *That can't be!*" gasped Frank.

His penis finished its journey to erection instantly.

He clicked to the next page. He was enthralled. He needed to know if what he saw was real.

It was. In this image, the dress hung the same way and the stance was similar, but "Sunny" had pulled the panties down and fished out her penis. It stood out straight, pointing right at the viewer.

Frank's jaw dropped.

This was a gorgeous woman. A gorgeous woman in a dress with amazing breasts and no traces of being a man, but there between her legs was a penis... an erect penis. Not just any erection either, but a classic erection. It was long and wide and solid and straight. It looked a lot like Frank's and it had to be at least as long as Frank's based on proportions or maybe even a hint thicker. And it was pointed right at him.

"That's — that's impossible," said Frank.

Frank stared at the penis in utter shocked. Was this some photo manipulation trick? It couldn't be real, could it? What if it was? He felt a strange chill race down his spine and he now noticed for the first time that his hand had latched onto his own erection and was stroking him earnestly.

He had even begun to breathe hard.

Frank pressed the link to see the next picture. "Sunny" now lay on a couch with her penis and breasts exposed as before. She was very erect; Frank could see how long the shaft was from this angle and he saw two of her fingers with pretty red nails holding the shaft from the bottom and her thumb pressing it from the top as she stroked it. She leaned on one elbow. Her head was thrown back exposing her throat. One leg ran off the couch to the floor, where the heel of her pump was jammed into the carpet. She'd brought her other foot up next to her erection with her leg folded. He stared at the erection.

"That's incredible," he gasped in disbelief.

He stroked faster.

Frank studied the image. He couldn't believe how exciting this was. "Sunny" had been exciting as a woman for sure, but the contrast of all her femininity with the stiff manhood jutting? It was... it was — uh —

A cold chill raced through Frank. Warning bells screamed inside his head. He was staring at another man and stroking himself! A *man*! A *penis*! That was unacceptable!

Frank pursed his lips, dramatically yanked his hands from his erection and recoiled from the image. He slapped the laptop closed and jumped up from the chair. His erection swung around the room, refusing to deflate. He refused to touch it.

"I— what—"

He shuddered.

"I didn't— I wouldn't—"

Frank took several deep breaths and told himself it had all been a mistake. He didn't know "Sunny" was really a man or he wouldn't have looked. It had all been "research." It was all the stress he felt, that was all. This didn't really turn him on. No, it didn't.

But he knew it had.

—o—

That night, Frank had a dream. Rather than wearing the pink shorts and the loafers, Frank saw himself dressed as "Sunny," complete with the enlarged, perfect breasts and the long, stiff erection. In this dream, he lay on the bed stroking himself as Martha took photos of him and giggled.

"You're the perfect girl now," she said.

Frank shuddered with excitement and stroked harder.

"Let's get ready for our dates," she said.

Frank woke up with a start. He was sweating. He was hard as a rock too. Fortunately, he had not come, though that may have been the least of his concerns at that moment; why had he dreamed this? Frank glanced at his wife sleeping next to him. She was smiling as she slept quietly. He wondered what she was dreaming and what she would say if she knew about his dream. He needed to fix all of this and fast, he told himself.

Chapter Ten: "A Hard Day"

— o —

Today would prove hard for Frank, in many ways.

When Frank awoke, Martha was already almost completely dressed for work. She wore a dark gray suit with a tight knee-length skirt and a white blouse. Her legs were covered in tan hose. Her feet were bare. She was slipping silver earrings into her ears.

"Good morning, sleepy head," said Martha.

"Morning," said Frank.

"I laid out your clothes for the day," said Martha and she motioned to the clothes she wanted him to wear, which had been laid out on top of their dresser. This included the pink shorts he had tried on, a pair of pink cotton panties, the white top with the spaghetti straps and the dark red loafers. He cringed when he saw those and his pride burned within him, telling him to fight this. But he had already lost that battle and he knew fighting it again would be pointless as there was no alternative until he got new male clothes.

"How about I just go nude?" said Frank sardonically.

"If you want to answer the door naked, that's up to you."

Frank scoffed. "I am *not* answering the door today, certainly not in those!" He pointed at the clothes his wife had laid out.

Martha shrugged her shoulders. Then she slipped her feet into her black stilettos, growing several inches taller in the process. "Since you'll be home all day, I'd like you to clean the house."

Martha had done all the cooking and cleaning until she got the job at the medical clinic. Now that she worked all day, she'd asked him repeatedly to help out around the house since he normally spent the day home doing nothing before work. Frank had been hesitant to do housework, however, as he saw that as his wife's responsibility; plus, the idea of him doing the housework made him feel oddly creepy – it challenged his manhood. So he invented excuses to avoid it, like needing to run errands for work such as finding specialty alcohols for the bar – he was assistant manager and head bartender after all, so it seemed plausible. Now that he really couldn't leave the house, however, Martha knew there were no excuses.

"Me?" he grumbled.

"Yes, you'll be home. I'll be working. You might as well make yourself useful."

"How do you know I don't have somewhere to go?"

Martha raised an eyebrow and chuckled at her husband. "And where are you planning to go?" she asked conspicuously glancing at the feminine clothes and then at his disturbingly androgynous (or worse) form.

Frank took her point and remained silent. A slight blush gave away his thoughts.

For her part, Martha nodded her head as if accepting her victory. She shrugged on her navy blue suit jacket. "Do the floors and the kitchen. I'll handle the laundry since you don't know how." She grabbed the bag of his clothes that needed to be tailored. "I'll take these to Rosalie on the way to work."

They kissed and she left.

—o—

Frank lay in bed for some time before he could convince himself to get up. He dreaded getting out of bed. Or, more accurately said, he dreaded getting dressed. He thought long and hard about going naked or just trying to wear his own clothes, but he knew he was being silly. Was his ego that weak that he couldn't handle some feminine shorts for one day? No one would see him after all!

He sighed.

Frank threw off the blanket and picked up the silky top first. It was so feminine. Why didn't his wife have something a little more masculine? The material was feminine. The lightness of it was feminine; you could almost see through it. And the spaghetti straps were super feminine. Frank shuddered. Men should not wear shirts like this, he thought. In fact, he again debated going shirtless.

"Maybe I will," he said.

Frank reached for the shorts and panties instead and slipped into those. The panties were worse than the top, but at least they would be hidden. The shorts... they weren't great, but ultimately they could be men's shorts except for the color. He could bear that.

Frank moved to the mirror to examine himself.

"Ug," he said immediately.

Without the top, he looked like a small-breasted, topless young woman. Indeed, the first thing he noticed, looking at himself, was the appearance of two small but obvious breasts hanging from his chest and jiggling when he moved. That was an unavoidable sight. He burned with embarrassment as he imagined his wife smugly saying, "I told you so." Without a second's hesitation, he grabbed the top and pulled it over his torso to hide his shame.

It didn't help much.

For one thing, the top did nothing to contain or steady the mounds. Their constant movement reminded him they were there. Moreover, the top was so thin he could still see their shape through the shirt for the most part. Even worse, the thin material let his areolas show through just slightly, making him feel disturbingly feminine. At least, he thought, once his clothes were tailored, he'd be able to hide this behind a heavy shirt or his vest for work. But in the meantime, this was it. He vowed that no one would see him dressed like this. *No one.*

Frank slipped into the loafers. They made him a little taller than his normal loafers, but otherwise didn't feel too different. Oddly, the extra height seemed normal to him. He suddenly realized that this meant he had gotten shorter! That wasn't really possible, was it?! If so, how short could he get? Could he become smaller than Martha? That would be utter humiliation if he had to physically look up to his wife! The thought made his stomach drop and a sense of weakness crawled up his spine. His body trembled.

"I can't really be shrinking," he said to assure himself.

It didn't help.

Frank cautiously returned to the mirror now that he was fully dressed. He shuddered; his shape was definitely feminine. His hips were wider than his waist, his chest bulged out slightly and he looked soft overall. The clothes seemed to make this worse. His wife seemed to have picked the perfect things to make him look unmistakably feminine, as if she wanted to highlight the changes. He cringed.

Then something odd happened.

In the midst of his masochistic imaginings, his penis suddenly grew firmly erect, bulging out the shorts. What's more, looking at his feminized image began to arouse him. He tried to press his penis back into a flaccid state and failed.

"That's just what I need," he said unhappily.

Frank stared at his feminized body and dress in the mirror, and the contrast of his erection. To his surprise, he found this contrast highly erotic. He was stunned. He'd never once thought of men dressing as women as being exciting. If it came up at all, he'd just dismissed it as weird. But now, staring at his reflection, he actually found himself having a sort of fantasy over it. In it, he saw a young woman in panties and a bra and heels. She was gorgeous and petite and delicate. But this was no woman, or at least not entirely. She had an enormous erection pushing out her panties. Frank saw himself approach the woman. She pressed the sides of her breasts, inviting him to touch them. Frank ignored them, however, and focused on the woman's stiff penis. He pulled down the panties, letting it pop out. Then he reached for it —

"What am I doing?!" he gasped.

The dream girl disappeared.

Frank shook his head vigorously as if he could shake the memory of what he'd imagined out of his head. Then he forced himself to shudder as a statement of his own disgust. He couldn't believe what he'd just fantasized about. That wasn't him! Why would he imagine such a thing?! Frank took a calming breath. Then he glanced at his reflection again and nervously licked his lips. This was troubling.

"It must be all this," he said dismissively, waving his hand generally at his feminine attire. That sounded like a reasonable explanation. "Fortunately, it's just for today. I get my clothes back tomorrow."

Crisis averted. He still felt funny though... self-conscious.

"Wouldn't Martha laugh if she knew?!" he said sourly.

One thing was for sure, this was something he never wanted anyone else to know... *ever*!

—o—

As Frank started moving around the house, everything felt off to him. His "shirt" was too light. His shorts were too tight, and tight in the "wrong" places. His "briefs" were too snug around his balls and slipped into his crack. And "his" loafers seemed to put more pressure on his toes than they normally did. All of this conspired to make him uncomfortable, both physically and emotionally. His emotional disquiet came from knowing these things were not a shirt or briefs or his shorts or his loafers, and the reason he wore these instead of his own was that his body was morphing into something terribly embarrassing. That was a hard thing to accept.

Then there was the other problem.

When he reached the hallway and its wooden floors, he heard his heels strike the hard surface for the first time. They sounded like his wife's clogs when she walked around in them: *THUNK! THUNK! THUNK! THUNK! THUNK!* That sound sent an erotic shiver down his spine. It excited him.

Excited him.

How could that excite him, he asked unhappily?

What's more, with each heel strike, he felt his chest jiggle. It was the most disconcerting feeling because it wasn't a manly feeling at all; it was an anti-manly feeling, an incredibly feminizing feeling. It meant he had breasts now. Small. Not fully developed. But breasts. Women's breasts.

He felt incredibly girly.

Frank suddenly found himself with a raging erection at that thought.

He decided he needed to do something to distract himself. After all, he couldn't let himself be aroused by this. He saw himself very much as a man's man, and the idea of being aroused by turning into a woman threatened that! So he grabbed one of his favorite books. He picked a rather macho story about a rugged soldier during the Napoleonic wars. He figured he could lose himself in the book and then his thoughts of feminization would go away.

But it didn't work.

Try as he might, his mind just would not stop thinking about his feminization. He was hard as a rock, horny to touch it, and so distracted that he barely comprehended a word from what he was reading. And when he did, it often made things worse, like when the hero tears the dress off the maniacal countess exposing her breasts; all Frank could see was his own breasts growing larger and himself wearing the torn Empire dress the countess had worn and his erection popping out into the air.

He slammed the book shut and took a deep breath.

"I need to get my mind off this!"

But just mentioning "this" brought back a catalog of changes to his mind.

Frank took another deep breath, lay back on the couch, brought the book close to his face and started reading the words out loud to focus his mind. He reasoned that his mind could not drift off if he was reading aloud.

And so he read. And he read.

But he was reading about the countess and her firm heaving breasts... jiggly breasts. He read how she tittered off to her private room in her tall heels. THUNK THUNK, he heard the sound of his loafers or his wife's clogs and saw himself tittering off in her clogs... and then tall stilettos. The soldier followed and laughed. His wife became the soldier. "I told you so," she said smugly.

His erection throbbed.

He felt an intense desire to touch it. Not to stroke it, mind you. There was Dr. Amber's warning after all, but touching it did no harm, stroking it did. So he slipped his hand inside the shorts and the panties and tickled his shaft. It felt good, really good, better than ever actually. Suddenly, there was temptation to go further. Maybe he could give it a stroke... maybe two. But that was it.

"No more than that," he assured himself.

"But Dr. Amber didn't forbid playing, just coming."

"You can't stop in time."

"Of course, I can." He knew he was lying as he said it.

He stroked a little faster.

Frank twisted his lip. This was dangerous. "I need to stop," he said.

But he'd already made the decision to stroke himself to the point of coming, but no further. To him, that seemed to be the way to cheat the system. He could stroke himself all he wanted so long as he didn't push it too far, and he could judge that, right? Maybe he couldn't... but that seemed to excite him all the more: it added risk. This was like a game of chicken with feminization as the punishment for losing. That thought made him tingle and actually giggle, it felt so naughty. In fact, this was the naughtiest thing Frank could think of doing: to risk playing this game day after day, winning some and losing some, and the whole time secretly, slowly turning into a woman. He saw himself slowly growing breasts, right under his wife's nose without her even noticing. That actually turned him on! Then he saw himself prancing around the house in Martha's clothes when she wasn't home, again without her knowing, maybe even wearing some under her very nose. His penis was so incredibly hard!

He wanted this so badly. He started stroking himself faster.

He imagined Martha giving him suspicious looks. Was his chest a little bigger? Was his rear more curvy? Were his lips fuller? She wanted to accuse him, but she couldn't because she wouldn't know if it was really happening. And he would deny everything, of course! Only he would know when it would happen, when he would have a growth spurt... no, a "girl spurt."

Frank was breathing hard by this point in his strange fantasy. He spread his legs and stroked faster yet. More pressure. All it would take would be a little more pressure to make himself come, to take the next step. Or maybe go a tad faster. Again, that's all it would take to play this game. Maybe take that first step. Martha would never know what happened.

"I could have breasts," he giggled.

He slipped his free hand beneath the blouse and tickled his mounds. His nipples popped up. It felt so uncomfortable for them to pop up, but the discomfort was erotic in a way. It was exciting having nipples. Wouldn't it be even more exciting if they grew bigger?

"How big could they get before she knows?" he asked himself.

He felt his finger get wet. Precome had come. He needed to stop.

He stroked even faster.

"She'd never know. She thinks she knows everything, but she'd never know this! I could hide it from her easily." He felt smug. "Maybe I should do it!" He laughed as he said this.

He stroked faster yet.

Then he started to feel it. His muscles tightened. Something inside him started to pulse in rhythm. It felt like waves of joy pushing and pushing, but not quite finishing yet. This was a danger sign! He needed to stop and stop now!

He didn't.

He began to breathe harder.

"No one would know."

His breathing became erratic. "It would be my secret!" He was stroking so fast now. And then he felt everything stop for an instant in time. His breathing stopped. The rhythm stopped. The world stopped. He tensed up.

Then he heard Amber's words: *"Have sex, become a girl."*

But it was too late to stop. He exploded...

Frank's eyes shot open and he bolted upright in his seat. He was breathing hard, and he was sweating. His book was on the floor where it had fallen. He'd been asleep. He'd been dreaming. It hadn't been real. Relief flooded through him. Then he realized his hand was jammed inside his panties and he was holding his erection. Dr. Amber's words rang through his head: *"Have sex, become a girl."* And again: *"Have sex, become a girl."* Panic filled Frank. He yanked his hand out of his panties as if they were on fire. He examined it. It was dry. He had not done what he feared he had done. He breathed a second sigh of relief.

"What a nightmare!" he gasped.

Frank lay there trying to understand what had happened. Why would he dream such a thing, he wondered? He was a man. A man's man. He would never, ever, ever want that. Why would he ever want to turn himself into a woman? Worse, what if he had jerked himself off? He had apparently tried while he was sleeping. What if he tried again? How could he stop himself? How would he even know he was doing it until he woke up, and that would be too late? It seemed he had something new to worry about now.

Chapter Eleven: "Poker Night"
—o—

Frank spent the rest of that afternoon worried. The dream had shocked him and confused him. Was there something inside him that really did find this exciting or was this meant to be a nightmare? Looking just at the content of the dream, this should have been a nightmare. It should have been a warning about what was happening to him, i.e. that he was losing his manhood and he wasn't happy about it. Likewise, it seemed to include a warning that he thought his wife was encouraging his loss of manhood. Hence, a nightmare.

But then, why wasn't the dream more horrific if it was a nightmare? Why did it instead seem to be a sex dream, full of excitement and thrill? That didn't usually signify a nightmare. And if it was a warning, why did he seem to revel in it rather than fear it? So... not a nightmare? But if it wasn't a nightmare, then what was it? And if it had been a sex dream, then what did it mean? Why had he been fascinating by the woman's erection in the first part of the dream? The questions were troubling.

Frank was still struggling with these questions when his wife came home. She'd stopped at Rosalie's on the way home and picked up the clothes she'd dropped off that morning to be tailored.

"Finally," thought Frank with tremendous relief as he watched his wife come up the walkway. "Now I can put on men's clothes again and put all of this stupid craziness out of my mind. Goodbye girly shirt, goodbye girly shorts, goodbye girly loafers, and most of all, good riddance panties. I'll be happy if I never see another pair of panties in my life."

The door opened.

"Hello darling," said Martha as she walked through the door. Her purse hung over one shoulder as she carried the heavy bag of clothes with both arms before her as she struggled in her tall, narrow stilettos.

"Welcome home," said Frank.

Martha saw her husband in the skimpy top, the girl shorts and the ever-so-awkward loafers and almost giggled. She managed to hold it in, but she was sure the hint of a smile appeared upon her lips. She dropped the bag at Frank's feet and leaned forward to kiss her husband before setting her purse on a nearby table.

"Rosalie complained bitterly about the rush job, but she came through as always. She's the best," said Martha. "Unfortunately, it was expensive, more than we had, so our budget is tapped out at the moment."

"It was a lot of clothes," admitted Frank. "She did them all?"

"Everything you put in the bag. She said it took her all day, and I believe it."

Frank felt tremendous relief now that he could get back into male clothing. He picked up the bag – it was really heavy – and carried it to the bedroom. He was anxious to change. Martha followed him, stripping off her suit jacket as they went. Her high heels echoed off the hardwood floor of their hallway as they went, a sound Frank found oddly haunting suddenly.

"How was your day?" asked Martha.

"It was fine," lied Frank; he didn't want to tell

her about the disturbing fantasy or how strange he felt in her clothes or how the sound of her heels made him tingle nervously just now. "How was yours?"

"Busy but good."

Frank tore open the bag and started grabbing clothes. He felt almost desperate to change before his wife started asking him questions about how it felt to spend the day in her clothes. He snatched the first pair of pants he could find and he tossed those onto the bed next to him. Then he grabbed the pink shorts and all-but ripped them off. When they were on the ground around his ankles, he pulled down the panties and let them fall as well.

He was free. He was a man again.

Frank kicked both away from him and reached for the pants. As he did, he realized he needed underwear first, so he dove back into the bag... but he saw none. His stomach sank. Where were the underwear? Frank frantically dug to the left, to the right, and underneath, but he saw no underwear. He finally dumped the whole bag onto their bed. Shirts and pants spilled everywhere. But there were no underwear to be seen anywhere.

"What are you looking for?" asked Martha, who had just slipped out of her heels and was massaging her feet. She was watching him with an amused expression on her face.

"Underwear."

"You didn't put any in the bag."

Frank bit his lip. His wife was right; he had forgotten. He thought of shirts and pants, but underwear never occurred to him when he was virtually emptying his closet into the bags! That meant he had none now that would fit; when he'd slipped into his briefs the day before, they had fallen right off again.

"What do I do now?" he asked himself aloud.

Martha answered: "You'll just have to keep wearing the panties for now."

Frank swallowed hard. "Maybe I'll go without."

Martha smirked at Frank's insecurity. "Really Frank?"

Frank blushed. He was utterly embarrassed by the idea of wearing panties, but even more embarrassed that his wife knew he was embarrassed. Besides, what choice did he have? He imagined his manhood unhappily rubbing up against the zipper and he knew he needed to wear the panties. He wished he hadn't said anything and had just put them on. He had spoken, however. Now Martha knew of his discomfort.

Frank glanced around for the panties he had worn. Martha had picked them up and they dangled from her fingertip.

"Looking for these?" she asked.

Frank snatched the panties from his wife and slipped into them; he couldn't look her in the eyes as he did. As he pulled them back up his legs, the silkily snug feeling brought back all the disturbing thoughts he'd had this afternoon after the dream. It made him shudder... and it threatened to make him hard. He strategically turned his body away from his wife as he tried to tuck his penis into them to keep it down. It didn't help.

"I will never understand why panties freak guys out so badly," said Martha.

"I'm not freaked out," said Frank defensively.

Martha chuckled. "If you say so."

Frank ignored her and pulled his pants up as quickly as he could to hide the panties... and his growing erection. The pants fit perfectly. Rosalie had done an excellent job. He felt tremendous relief: he had pants again!

Meanwhile, Martha unbuttoned her blouse and hung it in her closet. She set her shoes in the closet as well. "Don't forget we're going to Tim and Kara's house tonight," she said.

Frank furrowed his brow. "What?"

"Tim and Kara's tonight."

"Why?"

"You boys are having poker night and we're doing a girl's get together upstairs," said Martha.

Frank pursed his lips. He didn't like the sound of that at all. Was this a good idea? With all that was happening, he really didn't want to leave the house. What if one of his friends noticed? Unfortunately, he knew he had no choice; Martha had already told him they weren't abandoning their social lives. He would just need to make sure that nothing feminine showed. To that end, he grabbed a heavy black collared shirt to replace his wife's flimsy top. Hiding his growing chest was key among his concerns. The heavy black canvas material of the shirt should hide a multitude of sins, he thought. And a glance toward the mirror confirmed it. His mounds were entirely hidden. He breathed a sigh of relief. Then he turned back to the pile of clothes to grab some shoes to replace the girly loafers... and realized there wouldn't be any; Rosalie was an excellent seamstress, but she couldn't make his shoes smaller.

"Uh— we don't have any shoes I can wear," he

said cautiously.

"Wear the loafers," said Martha in a matter-of-fact tone. She was looking through her closet for something to wear that night herself.

"But they—" he caught himself.

"What?"

"Nothing." He hesitated. "They pinch," he lied. What he really meant was that he felt incredibly girly wearing them because of their feminine red color and the feminine sound they made. He wasn't going to tell her that though as he already felt embarrassed enough without sharing details like that. "I'm buying new shoes tomorrow, and some underwear," he said as he slipped into them.

"Our budget is shot," said Martha.

"There must be some room."

Martha shook her head.

"Did Rosalie charge that much?"

"We took her whole day, Frank. She gave us a huge discount, but this was a lot of clothes you picked out for her to do. Maybe you should have been more selective than just cramming everything you had in the bag. Not to mention, we asked her to rush it. This cost a pretty penny, darling," said Martha. She then kissed her husband soothingly and started for the bathroom. "It's all right, darling. No one will think twice about the loafers."

Frank blushed. "They pinch, that's the problem!" he called after her defensively.

They both knew it wasn't.

—o—

Frank had never felt so self-conscious as when he walked through the door to Ted and Kara's home. The whole way coming up the walkway, he heard the sound of his wife's high heels clicking off the concrete and the sound of his own elevated heels "thunking" just a little abnormally. The closer they got, the more the "thunking" started to sound like Martha's heels too... or so it seemed. What's more he could feel the mounds on his chest jiggle beneath his shirt and he began to worry they might be visible after all. He even found the panties worrisome. Sure, they were hidden away under his pants, but they felt so tight around his balls that he wondered if they might not be creating pantylines to give themselves away.

"I should have gone without them," he lamented.

They reached the front door. Martha rang the bell. A moment later, Ted's wife Kara answered the door. She lit up and gave an over-the-top greeting to Martha before acknowledging Frank.

"The boys are in the basement," she said to Frank.

Kara stepped aside, allowing Frank and Martha into the house. She led them to the kitchen where the stairs to the basement were located. There, Frank saw Carl's wife Jeanette sitting at the kitchen table with a drink in her hand. She always seemed very bubbly to Frank. Frank smiled at her and she smiled back. As he did, Kara passed by him. At first, she seemed to ignore him – she often acted coldly toward Frank and Carl – but then she raised her eyebrow and she glanced at Frank out of the corner of her eye. Frank saw it. It was a strange look. Indeed, Frank would have sworn she glanced him up and down before letting out a sort of snicker or chuckle. She began to smirk.

Frank's stomach dropped. Was it possible she had recognized the loafers as women's loafers? Might she have seen pantylines? He decided not to wait to find out. Instead, he disappeared down the stairs to the basement as quickly as he could. A chill raced down his spine.

−o−

Frank felt sick to his stomach as he walked downstairs; his knees shaking. It would take him time to calm down from possibly being spotted wearing women's clothes. He knew this had been a bad idea and he dreaded what might happen next. Would Kara confront him? Mock him? Would she tell Ted? Would she tell Carl? Ted might understand. He would snicker, but he was a good guy. Carl? Carl loved playing the part of the macho jerk; he tried to out-manly each of them and challenged everyone's manhood, he always "talked tough" about women, he even married, forgive Frank for saying this, a bit of a bimbo. The prospect of Carl knowing he was growing breasts was sickening. He would totally humiliate Frank.

But as the minutes passed without Kara coming downstairs to tell his friends about his sissy sense of fashion, he slowly convinced himself that she had noticed nothing; it had all been paranoia. That calmed him a little. Interestingly, the passing of the intense sense of danger let his mind drift and he soon found himself tingling at the thought of the look on Kara's face. Indeed, the thought that she had seen his pantylines began to cause him an erection. He didn't understand why that would be. Why would being caught by her turn him on?

They were playing cards.

"Two pair," said Carl and he slapped down his cards. He'd won. He was winning a lot. Frank felt too sheepish being before his friends in women's shoes and panties and with an erection to put up much of a fight, he would rather go unnoticed this night. Ted too seemed out of sorts. That let Carl run wild through the deck.

"This is not my night," said Ted softly.

"Mine either," agreed Frank.

Carl took a swig of his beer. "What's wrong with you two tonight? You're acting like you're at a funeral. We should be having fun, drinking beer, talking about women."

Frank nodded his head. He knew he had been acting timid and sheepish tonight. The problem was, he couldn't overcome his fears and act normally. Why was he hard over wearing women's clothes?

"Speaking of women," continued Carl, who was carrying the conversation all by himself tonight, "there's this new girl at work. She's a honey. Total hottie. And let me tell you—"

"Let me guess, she has the most amazing breasts," said Ted indifferently.

Carl laughed. "How ever did you know?" He leaned forward as Ted collected the cards. "Seriously! She's got these enormous boobs, and they're firm like melons. It's like she's got cantaloupes under her shirt."

"Not watermelons?" asked Frank in the same

indifferent tone Ted had used. He knew Carl's routine well. Every new girl at the office had melons for breasts, often watermelons and legs that went on forever. Today, however, Frank wasn't in the mood to play along with Carl about breasts, not with "melons" of his own sprouting on his chest. So he treated Carl's comment like it was bravado and he hoped Carl would be too embarrassed to engage in his usual diatribe.

He wasn't.

"Ha ha," replied Carl snidely. "You don't like breasts suddenly?"

"My wife doesn't like me liking breasts, on other women at least," said Frank.

"I'd never let my wife tell me what I could or couldn't do."

"Really? What does your wife think about your obsession with this new girl's breasts?" asked Ted doubtfully, seemingly on Frank's side.

Carl furrowed his brow. "You too, huh? What is wrong with you two today? Do your wives have your balls in their purses? Well, *since you asked*, my wife is fine with me looking at other women's breasts."

"So she knows you're watching this new girl?" asked Frank.

"My wife knows I'm a man's man, and men look."

"And she approves?"

"Naturally," said Frank proudly.

"My wife would kill me if I looked," said Ted.

"That's because she has your balls in her purse," repeated Carl. He sucked down the rest of his beer.

"No, she doesn't!" snapped Ted. He spoke in a tone which seemed more defensive than usual for the ribbing the three friends always gave each other at their poker nights. Frank noticed, and assumed Ted and Kara must be fighting. Frank then thought about making some comment about Ted's balls to pile on and show that nothing was bothering him, but he felt a little uneasy taking shots at another man's masculinity given what was happening to him. Fortunately – or perhaps unfortunately – he was saved before he needed to say anything by the sound of three pairs of high heels tottering down the stairs.

The girls were coming to the basement. Frank tensed up.

"Hi boys," said Kara as she popped out of the staircase. "Are you all playing nicely?"

"Yes, dear," responded Carl with a laugh and he winked at Ted.

Ted glared at him.

"We thought we'd come check on you," added Martha as she appeared next.

"I wanted to see if you'd won me anything yet," joked Jeannette. "Mama needs a new pair of Louboutins."

"Any minute, baby, any minute," said Carl.

As each woman fanned out to her husband, Martha came up behind Frank and draped her arms over his shoulders. She let one hand droop down over his chest, as she always did in this posture. Normally, this wasn't a problem. Normally, her hand brushing against his chest felt nice but nothing more. But things were not normal at the moment. At the moment, Frank was growing breasts... sensitive breasts. So when her hand pressed against his mound, his nipples popped up under the shirt and the whole mound began to tingle. His penis shot to attention too and became rock hard. He even found himself sucking in a tense breath. He was highly aroused.

"Red eight on the black seven, honey," said Martha.

"No helping," blurted out Carl with a laugh and everyone laughed. Everyone except Frank, that is. Frank's mind was elsewhere.

Martha began swaying gently back and forth behind him – she must have had a couple drinks, he thought. In so doing, her hand slowly brushed over his erect nipple, just barely touching it. Frank started to breathe more heavily. Then she started absentmindedly massaging his mound with her fingers. Then her fingers found the nipple and she started toying with it, as one might a pencil or coin. It was clear she didn't realize the effect she was having on him. She ran a single nail across it. This sent a shocking jolt of pain and pleasure racing through his body all the way to the tip of his penis; it even made his toes curl.

Frank's breathing became labored and jagged.

His erection started to throb inside the panties. He could feel the panties become damp as precome dripped out into them. His mind flashed to Dr. Amber's words: *"Don't come."*

"Is precome the same problem?" he worried.

He didn't know.

Frank immediately thought about shooting out of his chair and throwing off his wife's hand, but he knew that would be a huge mistake. That would tell everyone something was wrong; then he would need to explain! Heck, it might even surprise Martha and make her blurt out what had happened, especially if she was a little tipsy. So he couldn't risk that. Unfortunately, hints probably weren't going to help either. Martha seemed oblivious and if she was tipsy, offering hints again risked the chance of an outburst. Besides, what hint could he give that wouldn't give away there was some reason he didn't want his wife touching his chest... his girly chest.

"Give me two," said Ted.

Carl tossed Ted two cards. As he did, Martha's fingers swirled around the nipple's edge touching it gently. Each touch made Frank shudder and throb. His panties got wetter. His throbbing became more rhythmic. He was getting closer to disaster... closer to feminization.

"So what were you boys talking about down here?" asked Kara.

"Boobs," said Ted pointedly and he shot a look at Carl which said, "You said it. Let's see you back it up."

"Whose boobs?" asked Kara.

Ted smirked. "Go ahead," he said to Carl.

Carl glared at him. "I have no idea what you're talking about."

"You better be talking about mine," said Jeannette in a half-joking tone before adding, "and you better be saying great things."

"Always," laughed Carl. He kissed his wife's lips over his shoulder.

Frank's breathing was becoming erratic. He was struggling to hide it. Martha's doodling finger was driving him crazy, especially whenever her nail scraped against the newly-sensitive material. Between the pain and shock of that, and the incredible pleasure that came with the caress of her soft warm fingers, he was on the verge of a massive eruption. Indeed, his erection had gone from throbbing to thrusting into his panties. And second and it would happen.

"I'll take one," said Ted.

"One set of balls," grumbled Carl. "I hear they're in your purse, Kara."

"For safekeeping, yes. Where does Jeannette keep yours, Carl?" laughed Kara snidely.

Everyone laughed, except Carl... and again Frank.

Frank was on the verge of coming. He didn't know how to stop it though. His penis was throbbing in rhythm. His muscles tightened. Then it hit him. He'd been so slow, his mind focused on his worries that he'd failed to see the solution. It was so simple too! All he needed to do was grasp his wife's hand and hold it; stop the source of pleasure! He folded his cards and reached up to take his wife's hand.

It was too late though.

Halfway to his wife's hand, his breathing stopped. He tensed up completely. His muscles seized up. His penis thrust forward. And then it exploded. One, two, three blasts of precious male hormones shot out of his body into his pink panties.

Frank collapsed, becoming very limber. It had felt amazing, but at what cost. He sighed.

"Are you all right?" asked Martha.

Frank stared at her for a second. He said nothing. There would be no point. What would he say anyways? He merely nodded his head. He would see what the morning would bring.

—o—

Frank lay awake that night feeling deeply embarrassed. His embarrassment had grown the more he thought about what had happened. It wasn't even that Martha had made him come that bothered him, it was *how* she had made him come. His wife had somehow jerked him off without ever touching his penis. She did it just by playing with his nipple with her fingers. That was something that had never happened to him before. Honestly, it had never happened in the recorded history of manhood as it wasn't something that happened to men. *It only happened to women!* What did that say about him that he had come in such a womanly way? How much had he changed already? The thought made him feel girly and weak.

"At least she doesn't know what she did," he thought. That would make it all worse.

Even worse, though, now that he had come, would he become even more feminine?

On the one hand, Frank didn't want to believe it. He told himself Dr. Amber's theory wasn't true. It seemed impossible to him. What could be a more manly act than coming? How could that make him feminine? Oh, he knew the theory. Dr. Amber had explained it to him. But he just didn't believe it could be true. But what if it was? Would his nipples become larger? More sensitive? Would the mounds grow? They had taken his measurements the prior day to have his clothes tailored. Maybe, he thought, it would be a good idea to double-check his measurements in the morning.

"That could prove Dr. Amber wrong," he said bravely, but inside he was worried.

Frank glanced over at his sleeping wife. The idea of becoming feminine – turning into a woman, was embarrassing. He could maybe handle it if no one ever knew: "If I lived in a cave somewhere," he thought facetiously. But his wife knew. She had already seen the traces. She would see more if it happened, the growing breasts, whatever else was happening. She might even see his penis shrink!

"What if it gets tiny?" he asked with a shudder.

He imagined his wife holding a tiny child-sized penis in her palm and laughing at him. "I told you so," she would say.

He shuddered again. But at the same time, his penis grew hard at the image.

"Traitor," he grumbled.

Frank spun over onto his side and buried his penis between his thighs. He didn't want to think about it. Then he closed his eyes and told himself this was all a nightmare. Everything would be normal in the morning. At least, at a minimum, nothing would have changed tonight.

He was wrong.

When he awoke in the morning, he was determined to measure himself to prove nothing had changed. He told himself he was certain nothing had. So he grabbed his pants from the night before – the ones Rosalie had taken in. His wife had put the notes with his measurements on them in her purse. The tape measure was in a drawer in the living room. He needed those. He would grab those and then put this stupid idea of Dr. Amber's to bed. He slipped his feet into the pants and pulled them up his legs. When he pulled them up now, however, they hung loosely on his waist. His stomach dropped. They had fit perfectly the night before!

It seemed, Dr. Amber had been right.

"Now what?" asked Frank and he swallowed hard.

"*Don't come,*" came the reply from Dr. Amber's voice in his mind.

Chapter Twelve: "Hiding It"

—o—

Frank was nervous about going to work the next night. He hadn't been spotted the prior night at Ted and Kara's house as far as he knew, but it had been close. Then there was the fact he was smaller again this morning, as shown by the new clothes not fitting. That probably made it all the more visible. There was no doubt he was changing anymore. The question was: could other people see it yet?

He shuddered at the thought.

"Imagine if Jade can see it," he thought.

Then he thought back to the strange look Kara had given him. Had she seen pantylines? Was that why she looked at him so oddly? What if he had them now? He checked himself in the mirror a dozen times as he dressed for work, but he couldn't see himself in a way to know for sure if he had them or not. What if they were only visible from a distance or directly from behind or only when he bent over? He couldn't tell that from a mirror. Other people could, if they looked.

"A lot of women check out men's butts," he said nervously.

He suddenly had the nightmarish vision of someone calling him "miss." That thought made him shudder, but it oddly seemed to excite him too.

"This is terrible," he said.

The idea of getting caught was terrifying, but it wasn't even what bothered him the most. He was awash in insecurities at the idea of losing his masculinity. The fact his clothes had become looser meant his muscles had shrunk. He was clearly smaller and weaker. His mounds had probably grown too; he couldn't bring himself to check. That meant he *was* growing breasts – though he would never accept the word. At least they would be hidden beneath the tight vest he wore for work, but he would still know they were there... soft, firm and girlish, oh so girlish. And what if they bulged out the vest so people noticed? Would people see him as a man or a woman or something humiliating in between if he looked weaker and had two bulges on his chest?

He wanted to stay home, but he had no choice.

— o —

Frank worked from six to midnight tonight. He set his wallet and phone into a small locker in the employee break room. Evelyn, one of the waitresses, was putting her street clothes into one of the larger lockers. The larger lockers were used mainly by the waitresses so they could keep a "uniform" dress or two at work and change in the employee break room rather than wearing their dresses home. The dresses they wore were rather fancy and did not lend themselves to commuting. Evelyn's street clothes had been tight jeans and sneakers. The dress she wore now was dark-emerald-green in color and made of satin.

"Looks like a busy night," she said.

"It does," replied Frank cautiously. He was waiting tensely for her to notice the way he looked. She didn't say anything though. Perhaps she didn't notice? Could that be?

"Hopefully, the tips are good," she added.

"Hopefully."

Evelyn sat down on a bench and slipped her feet into her shoes. These were strappy golden sandals with four-inch stiletto heels. Hardly the stuff of normal restaurants, but standard practice for *Empirey*. She noticed him glancing at her high-heeled shoes.

"You're lucky," she said as she threaded the ankle strap of her right shoe through its corresponding buckle.

"How's that?"

"Because you don't need to wear these things. They may be beautiful, but after a six hour shift, they'll kill your feet."

Outwardly, Frank remained calm; he nodded at her comment but otherwise shied away from responding. Inwardly though, his heart was racing with terror because he had already technically worn heels, i.e. the loafers, and he was still wearing them. And if by some chance she recognized that, he was going to be humiliated! Not to mention, William would probably fire him if he knew Frank was wearing women's shoes, given how William was. Frank felt like he would throw up at the thought. Hence, he excused himself, and he fled to the bar.

Frank felt much more calm behind the bar. This was his domain. He was in control here. But it didn't make him entirely immune to his nerves. The restaurant was extremely busy tonight. More people meant a greater chance of being discovered, so Frank remained tense as he watched for any sign of trouble. Unfortunately, this made time pass incredibly slowly for him as he kept one eye on the clock hoping his shift would end.

As the night progressed, however, and no one

seemed to notice anything unusual about him, Frank started to calm down. That said, every time he saw Jade, he went right back to being super-nervous. The reason was their natural state of conflict, compounded with his absolute horror at what would happen if she sniffed out the slightest hint of what was happening to his masculinity. Worse, she seemed to be watching him for some reason tonight. That made him insecure, though he knew this was most likely his imagination. He felt paranoid about being outed for his increasing femininity and he knew that was making him see suspicion in her every glance, when she likely hadn't seen anything. If she had, he tried to tell himself, she would have said something already. She never missed a chance to insult him in some way; she couldn't resist it. In fact, he'd just about convinced himself that his fears were overblown when his boss William came to the bar.

"How's the bar looking?" William asked. He meant the receipts.

"A little ahead of normal," said Frank.

William nodded his head. Then he peered over Frank's shoulder and he groaned. Frank turned to see Jade approaching. She wore a black cocktail dress and black strappy high-heeled sandals tonight. She was quite gorgeous actually.

"Here comes trouble," said William.

"I want to talk to you," growled Jade at William as she approached the bar. She pointed at Frank. "Two gin and tonics," she said. Then she returned her focus to William. "When are you going to let me tend bar?"

"Why do you want to tend bar?" asked William.

"There's more money in it. So when are you

going to let me do it?" demanded Jade. Her tone was aggressive, but still just professional enough not to be called insubordination.

"When you grow a dick," said William.

Jade turned bright red with anger and shock. Her jaw dropped. William, on the other hand, seemed proud of the effect his comment had on Jade. Frank, however, decided this was the perfect moment to duck down behind the bar, out of the line of fire, pretending to grab a fresh bottle of tonic water from a small refrigerator he kept beneath the bar.

"I should sue you," snapped Jade sharply.

"Over this lousy job? I think not." William then glanced down at Frank, who was only now returning to his full height. He noticed Frank's loafers. "Those aren't part of the uniform," he said.

Frank's heart stopped. Had William seen his pantylines? "W— what isn't?"

"Dress shoes with laces only, no slip-on shoes."

"Sh— shoes?"

"No loafers. And why aren't they black. They look kinda red."

Frank both breathed a sigh of relief and bristled with terror. William hadn't spotted his panties, that was true, but he had spotted his shoes... women's shoes. And he realized their color was wrong. Was he on the verge of realizing they weren't men's shoes? Frank held his breath.

"I— I'll change them," he squeaked.

As Frank said this, Jade leaned over the edge of the bar and glanced down at his shoes. That same curious look she had been giving him all night crossed her face once more, making Frank incredibly uncomfortable. Had she spotted what they were? Did she know something?

William turned back to Jade. "You wanna tend bar? I'll think about it," he said and he walked off.

Jade grunted and walked off too. She did not mention Frank's shoes.

Chapter Thirteen: "More Problems"
—o—

The following day, Frank ventured to his wife's closet. This was honestly the last place he wanted to be – it made him nervous and made him feel funny, somehow – but he had no choice. With the clothes Rosalie took in getting noticeably looser already, he wanted to see if he could find some sort of masculine shirt and maybe some jeans that fit or something that could pass for men's clothes. Also, with William's threat about the loafers and them having no money whatsoever at the moment, he hoped to find something to replace the loafers. Maybe, he hoped, his wife had something that looked more like men's dress shoes.

Naturally, she didn't.

His wife had a lot of heels though. She liked heels. She had some sneakers too, but they were pink. Pink would not do. She had some sandals, but they were mainly wedges. And she had flats, but they looked far more feminine than the loafers. Women simply didn't wear oxfords or wing tips, and when they did, they tended to have giant heels. Indeed, Martha had a pair just like that, but there was no chance Frank was going to wear those.

Frank sighed.

He then looked through his wife's jeans. The problem here was that most were capris or tight cut with feminine adornments, like rhinestones. They would stand out for sure.

"I need something," he said unhappily as he pushed his way through her clothes.

Ding dong.

The doorbell rang.

Frank left the bedroom and went to answer the door. When he opened it, he saw Kara standing on their porch. She was holding a white pastry bag. She wore a copper miniskirt, a black top, and black open-toed pumps with tall heels. His stomach jumped into his throat. Why was she here?

"Hi Frank," she said.

"Hi Kara," said Frank cautiously with some surprise. "Martha's not here."

"Oh, I know," she said dismissively. She then walked past him and made her way to the kitchen without even asking. Her high heels echoed off the hardwood floor as she went: *CLICK! CLICK! CLICK! CLICK! CLICK! CLICK!*

Frank chased after her.

"Can I help you with something?" by which he meant, "What are you doing uninvited in my house?!"

She held up the pastry bag over her head as she kept walking. "Just dropping off some cookies from a new shop for Martha. She asked about these the other night." She slipped into the kitchen and set them on the counter. Then she turned and leaned her rear against the counter. She pressed her heel into the floor and wiggled her foot suggestively.

Frank watched her with an odd sense that she wanted something. This was all very tense. Why was she really here? Was it the pantylines after all? Could that be what brought her here? He told himself to remain calm, but he was struggling. "I— I'll be sure to tell her."

Kara smiled, but it was a crooked smile. A no-good smile. "How are you, Frank?"

"Me? I'm good." His voice betrayed his nervousness.

Kara pushed herself away from the counter. She aimed herself at him. "I hope you enjoyed your time the other night, visiting with Ted."

She definitely wanted something. "I— I did."

"Good," she said and she took a step closer.

"I— I hope you did too," said Frank.

Kara's smile sharpened, if that was possible. She stepped closer now. She was within reach. Then she stepped right up to him and she leaned forward as if she wanted to whisper in his ear. Frank froze.

"I love your shoes," she whispered.

"M— my shoes?"

"Your loafers." She paused. "I have a pair just like them at home."

Frank's brain saw fireworks. Had she said what he thought she said? Had she realized he was wearing women's shoes?! Before he could say anything, she pressed her lips against his and kissed him deeply. As she did, she slipped her hand into his pants and panties, latching on to his erection. Frank stood there stunned, having no clue what to do, knowing only that this turned him on incredibly despite all his better judgment, but it scared him too. She then leaned forward once more and again whispered in his ears.

"Panties? You naughty boy," she purred.

She started stroking his erection. Frank felt his whole body tingle. He was incredibly aroused. So much so, in fact, that he could barely think to resist, and what resistance he could offer was token only.

"Please, don't—"

Kara ignored him and kept stroking. She kissed

his lips. "Why were you wearing Martha's shoes at my house?"

Frank felt so incredibly embarrassed. "I— I wasn't!"

"Yes, you were. Did Martha know?"

Frank opened his mouth but no sound came out.

"Are those her panties too? Does she know?" asked Kara breathlessly.

Frank felt dizzy. He had been caught! He had no idea how to answer. Yet, at the same time, he was somehow turned on. He was breathing hard. His body was trembling. His manhood was stiff and throbbing. He knew what was coming and he was both desperate for it to happen and desperate for it not to happen. Then he recalled what would happen if he came! He realized he needed to tell her, if she did this, he would become more feminine, but he was too embarrassed to tell her that. Not to mention, it probably wasn't a good idea to tell someone that! No, he couldn't tell her... but needed to stop her. Unfortunately, part of him wanted to come far too badly. It was like he knew what he needed to do, but he couldn't make himself do it.

"It— it was a joke," he said feebly.

Kara snickered doubtfully. "What else does she make you wear 'as a joke'?"

"N— nothing." He breathing became erratic; he was getting closer all the time. "I— I can't do this. Please, stop," he said.

Kara smirked evilly. This was far too juicy to stop. She stroked even faster. "I'll bet she has you prancing around in dresses and heels too, doesn't she?"

Frank shook his head. He tried to tell her to stop again, but the words wouldn't come; his brain was too conflicted. Something inside him did not want to stop. He closed his eyes. He was so close. He could feel the rhythm building. He wanted it so badly... except.

"Please," he said again, "stop. I can't. I really can't—"

"Of course, you can."

He shook his head. "You don't underst—"

And then she stopped. And then... everything stopped. It was jarring. The tingling stopped cold. The rhythm stopped. The amazing sensations stopped. It all came crashing to a halt as if he'd hit a brick wall. He felt a terrible, shocking feeling of utter, instant denial. His whole body shook, and in that moment, he desperately wanted her to finish what she had started regardless of what that meant.

She didn't though.

Instead, she stepped back, looked him up and down with hungry eyes, licked her lips, chuckled, and then she started toward the front door.

"You're— you're leaving?" he gasped.

"I'll be in touch," she said with a laugh.

"Wait! You— you can't!"

Kara laughed again and winked at him. Then she walked off.

Frank blushed. He had embarrassed himself, and now he watched her go despite that. Her high heels echoed her progress until she was out the door. At that point, he fell to his knees. He felt desperate for her to finish... but she hadn't. Why did he feel so desperate? Could the hormone imbalance have made him unusually horny? Or was it something else?

Frank swallowed hard. It seemed he had another problem.

Chapter Fourteen: "Martha Struggles"

—o—

While Kara played with Frank, Martha had gone to see Amber to find out more about Frank's condition. Amber had called her and said there was news which they should discuss. She found Amber sitting in her office going over files for various patients. Amber invited her to sit down, which she did, across the desk from Amber. She smiled politely as she always did when speaking to patients to put them at ease.

"You said you have news," said Martha.

Amber nodded her head. "I've been running tests. It seems the drug is more potent than I first realized."

"What does that mean?"

"It might mean nothing—" started Amber in her best "calm" voice.

Martha cut her off. "Nothing?" she said doubtfully. She knew the "calm" voice doctors used on their patients.

Amber leaned back in her chair and folded her arms. She tapped her finger against her lips before she spoke. "It all depends on the speed of the process. If his male hormones can continue to block the drug, then it could take some time for the changes to kick in."

"What is 'some time'?"

Amber shrugged her shoulders. "It could take years for any real effects to show. They will come, but it could be years."

"That's if his hormones do their job."

Amber nodded her head. "Correct."

"And if they don't?"

"If they don't, then things will be worse."

Martha ran her tongue over her lips nervously. "Worse how?"

Amber rose from her chair and came around the desk. Like Martha, she wore a below-the-knee skirt and open-toed pumps. Her nails were dark red, whereas Martha's were pink. She slipped her rear up onto the edge of her desk and folded her arms across her chest.

"Do you remember how I told you that he'll develop secondary feminine characteristics? I said: higher voice, loss of muscle tone, soft erection, gynecomastia – boy breasts. Well, I was wrong. I've never seen anything like this before, but if I had to guess, he'll start to develop actual feminine characteristics: genuine breasts, feminine muscle tone, soft, light female voice."

Martha's jaw dropped. "He'll turn into a woman?"

"Except his penis. That seems to be growing actually."

"So he'll become some sort of – of –"

"Shemale."

The moment Amber said it, something inside Martha quivered. She told herself this was an emotional response to the agony of what was happening to her husband, but she knew better. It didn't feel like agony; it felt like arousal, deep, intense, arousal. She bit her lip to keep it from forming into an embarrassed smile. "How – how long are we talking?"

"If his hormones are overwhelmed. Say he can't resist having sex. In that scenario... months... weeks. The changes are strikingly fast."

Martha forced a frown upon her face and looked down at her polished toenail sticking out the front of her open-toed pump to avoid Amber's eyes. She wiggled her foot nervously. She couldn't believe how aroused she suddenly felt. The idea that Frank could have actual breasts, look like a real woman, and yet have a fully-functioning penis... why did this excite her so?

She was wet.

"What's wrong with me?" she asked herself.

"How are you holding out?" asked Amber.

"Me?" blurted out Martha in surprise. She flushed with embarrassment, sure that the question was related to all the signs of horniness she was giving off. "I'm — I'm fine."

"I'm always here if you need to talk about it," said Amber.

And then she placed her hand upon Martha's knee.

Martha flooded her panties. She saw images of herself standing up and kissing Amber right then and there. In her mind, she felt Amber's hand upon her rear and her lips upon her own. And then... then she saw Frank in a dress with a massive erection watching them kiss. Her heart raced like mad at the image. Was she a lesbian? Did she want her husband to become a woman? Or was she just infatuated with Amber, but not really "interested" interested, if that made sense. She didn't know. She was so confused. She felt desire, arousal, and guilt all swirled together.

"I'm always here," repeated Amber.

As she said this, she placed her hand on Martha's shoulder. Then she let her hand slip down, following Martha's bra strap until it reached the top of her bra. Martha instinctively grabbed her hand and held it in place, keeping it from moving further, but not rejecting it either. Her nipples were painfully hard; that had rarely happened, if ever. An intense warmth radiated out from her lower region. She was so incredibly turned on. But she was conflicted too. She absolutely did not want to be disloyal to Frank, but was it cheating to be with another woman rather than a man? What if it was just a fling? Did it matter that she couldn't have sex with him? She suddenly felt an overwhelming need to leave the room before she did something stupid, and she didn't know what that would be.

"I— I need to get back to work," she said and she shot to her feet.

Amber nodded her head. She was back in clinical mode. "I'll let you know the moment I hear anything more."

"Th— thank you."

"Just remember, Frank can't ejaculate. You need to avoid sex with him," said Amber.

Martha didn't respond. She had reached the limit of her will power. She raced outside to the elevator back to her floor before she did something she would regret with Amber. She leaned against the elevator wall breathing hard as it started back upstairs. Her panties were soaked. A million thoughts raced through her mind. She was so incredibly horny she needed Frank... but Frank could not help her.

—o—

Later that night, both Frank and Martha lay in bed, in the dark, each wide awake. Neither could sleep. Neither knew the other was awake. Frank couldn't get the incident with Kara out of his mind. She had turned him on so intensely that he almost stroked himself to orgasm after she left him high and dry, even knowing the consequences. He was still stunned how excited that had made him and how overwhelming his desire had been. How could he almost beg her to make him come knowing it would turn him more into a woman? That was shocking. And then to almost do it to himself? Wow. Even wore, he knew this wasn't over. She had basically blackmailed him based on her knowing that he had been wearing women's clothes! She wasn't just going to walk away from that.

Martha couldn't sleep either.

At first, she kept thinking about Amber. She kept thinking how beautifully Amber's breasts curved and how her warm, soft hand felt against her body. She kept wondering why Amber excited her so. But in the middle of that, a strange thought hit her, the same she had in the office: she found herself wondering how Frank would look in a dress. Only, this wasn't the Frank she knew today; it was a Frank who looked a little more like Amber, a Frank with large breasts and wide hips and plump pouty lips. She felt so confused. What did all of this mean?

Martha closed her eyes and tried once more to fall asleep.

She seemed to doze off with visions of Frank with large breasts dancing in her mind. But then she was disturbed by a noise. She opened her eyes and saw Frank rise from the bed. He moved very quietly toward the closet.

"What's he doing?" she wondered.

As she watched, Frank ran his fingers over the line of dresses hanging in the closet. It was almost as if he was looking them over. Could he possibly be thinking what she thought he was thinking? He pulled one out, a simple yellow housedress and held to his body. She could see his erection through it.

"What are you doing, Frank?" she asked.

Frank jumped. "Me?" he asked nervously. She could almost hear him blush in the near darkness; only the moon provided light.

"Why are you in my closet?"

"I— I don't know. I was just looking to see if— I mean—"

Martha rolled out of bed and rose to her feet. She wore a dark-blue pajama set with loose pants. She slipped her feet into her wedge-heeled slippers. She moved to her husband and placed her hand on his back as he faced the closet. He wore a pair of pink panties and a loose pajama top that hung like a dress on him; his pajama bottoms no longer fit.

"Are you looking at my dresses?" she asked knowingly.

Frank shrugged an uncertain denial.

Martha arched her eyebrow; he *was* thinking what she thought! "Do you want to try one of them on?" Just the suggestion alone sent a ripple of energy through her and made her wet. She had images of Frank prancing around the house in a dress. Was she really turned on by the idea of seeing her husband in a dress? Could it be? And might it really happen?

"I— well," he stammered nervously.

Ann Michelle

Martha chuckled. "Oh my little sissy," she laughed. Then she hugged him from behind. She slipped one hand inside his panties and latched onto his stiff manhood. "My pwetty widdle husband wants to wear one of my dresses." She started stroking him slowly. "Which one do you like, darling?"

Frank withered, which made Martha chuckle again.

"It's all right, dear. I like the idea," she admitted.

"You do?" He sounded incredulous.

She nodded her head and kissed the back of his neck. "I do. We can get you all sorts of dresses and shoes and purses and you can become my secret girly lover. Everyone will think we're sisters, but really you'll be my husband hidden away beneath dresses and panties and bras." As she said this, she pinched his nipple and it rose like hers had. "We can even go on dates together. Would you like that, darling? You and I out with two men?"

Frank moaned.

Martha started stroking him, even though she knew she shouldn't do this. If she made him come, then he would turn into a girl, bit by glorious bit. Did she possibly want that, she asked? Maybe she did. The idea seemed to be making her hot. She wondered if her husband felt the same thing; he was hard as a rock and writhing beneath her touch. Maybe he did!

"Would you like that, darling?" she asked.

He was breathing harder now. His eyes were closed. His penis was throbbing in her hand,

"Would you like it if I gave you breasts?" she asked.

Frank gasped. "I don't want to be a girl!"

"But maybe I want you as a girl." She squeezed his erection tighter and stroked him even faster. She could feel his whole erection shake and vibrate in her hand. He was going to come. She could tell. And then... then he would grow more feminine. He was going to sprout breasts and become soft and small and girly, and he was going to be all hers to do with as she pleased! "I want you, Frank— I want you to be a girl."

As she said this, more visions of Frank in dresses and heels and makeup flashed before her eyes. She saw him with a whole feminine wardrobe and it fit him perfectly. She saw his erection sticking out of his panties. She stroked it. And then she saw him at a bar with her. They were the two hottest women at the bar. They were surrounded by men. The men were everywhere. They were all hard and horny with erections pressing out their pants.

It all faded.

Martha opened her eyes. She had been dreaming. She blushed as she realized what she had been dreaming. Oddly, a warm, happy feeling came over her next, not a shocked or horrified feeling. That surprised her. She should have been horrified at having a fantasy about her husband in a dress, so why wasn't she? She glanced at her husband sleeping next to her. As so often happened, he was hard and his erection pushed up his thin blanket. Martha leaned up on one elbow and carefully pulled back the blanket, exposing her husband's tented panties; they did nothing to hide his penis or control it. He wore them because his pajama bottoms no longer fit him... she was glad he did. She stared at his panty-covered penis.

"All I have to do is stroke it," she said beneath her breath.

She tingled all over at that thought. She was surprised how enticing that was. She ran two fingers along the panties, tracing his erection through them. Frank shuddered in his sleep as she did.

"He would never know."

She carefully pulled back his panties, freeing his erection. It wiggled tensely. He was excited. Then she very lightly ran her nail up and down the shaft. He shuddered again.

"He would never know," she said. "He would slowly become a woman, a little more every day, and he would never know why."

Martha ran her nail down his penis once more.

She stared at his erection longingly. It twitched. It was so ready. Should she help it along or not? She seemed to take an eternity to decide before reason took over from arousal. She could not do that to her husband, no matter how exciting it sounded. Finally, she pulled her finger away, though it took much more will power to do so than it should have. That made her bite her lip nervously.

Chapter Fifteen: "A Gift"

—o—

Frank watched his wife climb into her car in the driveway the following morning. She was going to work. She looked very pretty today... sexy, wearing a tight dress and extra-tall designer pumps. Not that she didn't look pretty every day, but the last week or so, it seemed to Frank, she had really dressed to impress.

"Trying to make a good impression," he assumed.

He still knew nothing of Amber's advances.

Either way, she was soon gone and his day began. Frank moved to the kitchen to clean up breakfast. His wife had cooked it, but left the dishes for him to clear away as he'd agreed to start doing chores around the house more regularly. He didn't like it, as it made him feel a tad emasculated to be doing housework, but he would do it; the men in his family had never really done housework. After all, he was going to be home all day while she was at work, so he had no real basis to object, and now was not the time to fight with his wife, not with everything going on.

So he would clean up.

Breakfast had gone well, with both acting seemingly chipper and normal, though Frank felt uneasy. He struggled with the issue of Kara. For one thing, he knew it wasn't over. For another, he didn't know if he should confess to Martha what had happened with Kara or if he should try to solve the problem himself. He knew it was usually best to tell his wife about things like this, but Kara was her friend and Ted was his friend and he didn't want to open that can of worms if there was still some chance to clear this up before it went anywhere.

"If she comes back— *and she might not,*" he told himself, but he knew she would. "Then I'll just tell her she's mistaken, that she has no proof, and that I would appreciate it if she would never mention it again."

Simple.

That was his plan.

What could go wrong?

"At least Martha seemed happy," he said, noting that she wasn't in her "I told you so" mode this morning for the first time in a week. To the contrary, she was all smiles, kissed him passionately and seemed to watch him with shy eyes. It reminded him very much of her moods after some romantic dinner date. That was a promising change, he thought. He didn't think to wonder what might have brought this change of moods on.

Frank put the dishes in the sink and returned the butter to the refrigerator.

Ding dong. The doorbell rang.

Frank glanced at the clock. It wasn't even nine o'clock yet. Who was visiting this early? He thought it must be a package. Frank looked down at the loose pajama tops and the pink panties that he wore; he had nothing else he could wear to bed and he owned no robe, so he'd worn this to breakfast. But he couldn't very well let some package delivery guy see him in panties!

"Can't answer the door in this," he said.

Frank walked to the bedroom and grabbed a towel. There wasn't time for anything more elaborate; besides but he wouldn't need anything more just to grab a package. He wrapped the towel around his waist to hide the panties as he walked to the front door.

It was Kara. Frank swallowed hard. "What does she want?" He thought about not answering it, but knew that would end poorly. He had to resolve this. So he opened the door.

"Well, hello," said Kara. "Nice towel."

Frank instinctively dropped his hand to cover the panties. He felt like a fool the moment he did it, however. Worse, the memory of her grabbing his member the last time and catching him in panties, made his penis grow long and hard, tenting out his panties and noticeably pushing the towel away.

"Happy to see me, Frank?" said Kara nodding at his obvious erection.

Frank blushed.

"You're— you're back," said Frank.

Kara nodded her head and pushed past Frank. She wore a tight, black knee-length dress and black pumps with high, sharp heels. Over her back, she carried a laundry bag which she held by the hanger over her shoulder.

"I come with a gift."

"A g— gift?"

"Yes, Frankie dear, a gift."

Frank took as deep a breath as he could to suck up his courage. He squared his shoulders and faced Kara as she started down his main hallway toward his bedroom apparently.

"Kara, listen," he said. "I didn't— I mean, there's no proof. We can't do this."

Kara glanced over her shoulder. The look on her face read somewhere between mild surprise, malicious intent, and joy. To Frank, the look screamed, "Oh, so you want to try me, do you?"

"Is that so?" she said.

Frank nodded his head, but his knees shook. Normally, he was confident and this should have been easier, but he was nervous about being exposed. What if she told his friends he'd worn women's shoes to the poker game or that she'd caught him in panties? They would never let him live it down, *never*! The fear of that made him weak and remarkably submissive even as he tried to project strength.

"I'm married," squeaked Frank.

Kara laughed. "I know."

She slowly moved toward Frank, one high-heeled step at a time. *CLICK*, pause, *CLICK*, pause, *CLICK*. That sound sent a shiver down Frank's spine adding to his weakness. Yet, it also made him incredibly horny. He didn't understand why weakness should be erotic?

"That just makes this all the more exciting," she purred.

"But it's wrong."

"It's naughty. Naughty is fun," countered Kara. *CLICK*, pause, *CLICK*, pause.

"Ted is my— my friend. Martha is your friend."

CLICK, pause, *CLICK*, pause. "All the better," said Kara. She took one last step and now stood inches from him, face to face. Her smirk spread across her face. "Oh Frankie, Frankie, Frankie. This is going to be so much fun."

Frank started to protest, but she put her finger to his lips to silence him. He stopped.

"I've brought you a gift, Frankie," she said.

"Wha— what kind of gift?"

"The best kind."

Kara slipped the laundry bag off her shoulder and pressed it to his chest. He took it from her. She then slid one hand down and latched onto the top of his towel before he could stop her. She yanked it away like a magician pulling away a tablecloth. His tented panties now stood out in the open air, hidden only behind the laundry basket. Frank tried to squirm behind it to hide the fact he wore panties, but it was hopeless; he looked foolish.

"Open it," she said.

"What is it?" he demanded.

"It's my gift to you."

"I don't want a gift."

Kara smirked. "Doesn't matter. I want you to have it."

Frank cast her a suspicious look. There really was no way out of this though, so he hesitantly pulled off the opaque plastic bag revealing a short black dress beneath. She had given him a dress! He blushed deeply.

"W— what's this?" he stammered.

"Put it on."

Frank shook his head. "There's no way."

"Unless you want me telling everyone everything, then you better put it on, and put it on right now," said Kara. Her tone was calm, yet made her determination unmistakable. He was going to wear that dress.

"Everyone?" repeated Frank nervously.

"*Everything.*"

Frank twisted his lips. She could do it. She

could tell his friends about the shoes and the panties. She could tell Martha how she had stroked him. Martha would believe it too if Kara thought to describe his panties. After all, there would be no other way for her to know about them except for seeing them. How would Martha react? Well, she wasn't in the best mood regarding Frank at the moment, that was for sure. And she'd made it clear she wasn't happy about being denied sex. If she learned that he'd let Kara stroke him? Well, that wouldn't end well, not at all. Then there was Ted. How would Ted react if he found out that his wife had played with Frank's package? That wouldn't go over well either and Frank doubted Ted would blame his own wife. These were problems. It seemed, he had little choice.

"Kara—"

"Put it on," she said, not even waiting for him to finish.

Frank bit his lip. He was beaten; he knew it. He slowly nodded his head. "All right," he said softly. This was going to be humiliating. It was going to be terrible. Frank pulled off his pajama top, leaving him only in the pink panties he was already wearing. Then he took the dress and unzipped it before sliding it over his head. He pulled it down into place.

And then... a funny feeling crept over him.

Frank was now wearing a dress. This was his first dress and he was rightly shocked. But he wasn't shocked for the reason he expected. He was shocked because as dangerous as the current situation was, as humiliating as it did feel, as much as his brain told him to run and never look back, he was incredibly turned on. He was a man... a man's man at that... and this...

this was arousing. He simultaneously trembled with humiliation and shook with giddiness. For an instant, one tiny milli-fraction of a second, he felt so incredibly turned on to be wearing a dress that he wanted nothing more than to beg Kara to make him dress like this forever. The thought was powerful, overwhelming and terrifying. It made him dizzy.

Then it passed. The shock was gone. The vision vanished, as did the desire to beg Kara to dominate him. His brain retook control. A general feeling of embarrassment came over him now instead. The erection stayed though. It was dripping with precome.

A slow smile broke out on Kara's face, both at him wearing the dress and the look of horror and exposure on his face. What was it he didn't want her knowing, she wondered?

"You look cute," she said.

Kara set her fingers on his belly before sliding them down the front of the dress, tickling his erection through the silky material as her fingers passed by. She reached the hem and lifted it so she could dip her fingers inside his panties. Frank knew he should resist, but he was still frozen from the uncertainty of wearing a dress. Kara wrapped her fingers around his shaft. She started stroking him. When she did, she did it lazily, slowly, but with the right amount of pressure. Indeed, the way she pulled on his shaft felt like she was tugging at his very soul with each stroke and whatever will he had to resist collapsed. Within seconds, Frank knew he was about to spurt out a fountain. And honestly, this time he was ready to let it happen.

But then that little voice inside returned. It reminded him of everything he had forgotten. If he let her do this, he would become more feminine. He risked growing breasts. Not to mention, Martha would be irate if she ever found out. Ted wouldn't be too happy about it either. Ted... the name seemed important.

"What about Ted?" asked Frank before he even realized it.

"What about him?" Her stroking slowed.

"He's not going to like it that you did this. You think you can blackmail me, but I can blackmail you too. I'll tell Ted that you seduced me and you jerked me off, twice." That seemed like the perfect threat to Frank.

Kara smirked. "You want to tell Ted?"

"I will."

Kara's smirk grew. Then she slipped her hand from his panties and turned and walked toward the door. Could she be leaving, wondered Frank? Had it worked? When she reached the door, she stopped. She put her hand on the knob, but then turned back to face Frank. Frank steeled himself against some threatening message.

"You want to tell Ted about this?" she repeated.

Then she snickered.

"By all means, be my guest," she said and she threw open the door.

Standing on the other side was a woman in an off-white dress with a brown purse strung over her shoulder and matching brown wedges on her feet. She had red nails and curly golden hair. Even more interestingly, the woman also had a bulge where women don't have bulges. More interestingly yet... that woman was Ted.

The End of Part One

— o —

Thanks for reading my book!
I hope you enjoyed it!

You can send me your thoughts at:
annmichelle@ymail.com

And, don't forget to check out my other books at my Amazon homepage:

https://www.amazon.com/Ann-Michelle/e/B007JLQ9RG/

Below are other Blue Label books you might enjoy!

— o —

Becoming Georgia (Blue Label Edition)

Poor George. George and his friend Oliver never meant to break the widow, but they did. Even worse, George's pesky stepsister Emma saw the whole thing. Now they would learn the price for her silence... and it included dresses. That's just the beginning too.

This is the tale of how George goes from average young man to feminized servant of his stepsister, to feminized maid for his ex-girlfriend and for the handsome boy who stole her from him, to finding himself going to the dance in the arms of another boy. Nothing will ever be the same for George again.

This was my first Blue Label Edition story. It is an alternate version of the original *Becoming Georgia*. This story is a little more graphic than the original because I think that's appropriate in this instance. It's different too, even as I tried to keep the original spirit of *Becoming Georgia*. Indeed, while this story starts the same and begins with only subtle changes, it slowly goes its own way to tell this story properly.

This is all four parts of the story in one volume.

For Mature Audiences Only. This 115,000 word story includes female domination, forced feminization, blackmail, male-to-male contact, bi, oral, spanking, and so much more!

March 2022 No. 1 Best Seller in Transgender Erotica at Amazon!

— o —

Feminization Island (Part Three) (Blue Book Edition)

In parts one and two, Walter was tricked into going on vacation at an island resort where he was feminized according to his wife's wishes. His "vacation" is now coming to an end, if you can really call it a vacation. It seems more like a job interview for a new position his wife is looking to fill: sissified husband. Either way, before things end, Walter is in for some major surprises. There's the rest of his training, the bachelor party, the wedding... that ring thing he forgot about. Good times! Do you think Jackie will make Walter wear a tux to the wedding after all? Probably not, right?

For Mature Audiences Only. This 34,957 word part is the third and final part of Walter's story. This is the Blue Book version ending to the story. This follows the regular Parts One and Two (so read those first) and then finish with this. Things get really kinky now. This part includes forced feminization, female domination, hormones, bondage, maybe-not-so-forced bi, chastity devices, power exchanges, a wedding dress and still more surprises! Walter's vacation pictures are going to be something special, that's for sure!

May 2022 No. 1 Best Seller in Transgender Erotica at Amazon!

— o —

Feminization For His Wife's Lover (Blue Book Edition)

George wants his wife Selena to sleep with another man. He doesn't understand why he wants this, but he knows the idea turns him on. Selena loves her husband and will do anything to make him happy, even this. But if she's going to do it, then she's going to do it on her terms. One of those terms involves George wearing a dress and panties while she dates this other man. This is the story of George and Selena's journey into cuckolding. If that bothers you, don't read it. If it doesn't, I think you'll find this to be highly erotic.

For Mature Audiences Only. This 33,500 word story includes female domination, power exchange, denial, cross-dressing, cuckolding, male to male contact, and so much more.

September 2022 No. 1 Best Seller in Transgender Erotica at Amazon!

Printed in Great Britain
by Amazon